I0773997

SPECTRUM

AN
AUTISTIC
HORROR ANTHOLOGY

Trigger warnings are listed at the back of the book.

Exterior formatting and illustrations by Jonathan La Mantia

Interior formatting by Katherine Silva

Edited by Aquino Loayza and Lor Gislason

ISBN 979-8-9868455-5-5 (Paperback)
ISBN 979-8-9868455-4-8 (Digital online)
First paperback edition April 2024
Published by Third Estate Books
https://www.thirdestatebooks.com

STORIES

WORRY YOUR HEAD

RAIN CORBYN

"Shit honeymoon," says your husband's severed head.

"Glad you can muster jokes," you reply, peering through the black rain beating on your carriage. The two of you can't see past your feeble horse, who drags a burden meant to be pulled by two. The downpour scrambles your hearing, same as your sight, but that's a problem you don't share with your husband. One secret of many. You reach for your rosary, then remember that after what you did, it withered, umbilical, on your chest.

Instead, you catch a raindrop and rub every grain of its inky silt between your thumb and finger. On the driver's bench, your husband's head resides in an open box, though, of late, you wish it would do more *resting* and less *gabbing*. He looks at you, and you shift your eyes to the road. He caught you looking, though.

"Well, I'm sorry you *can't* muster a joke. At least a laugh at mine! You're the one with a body. Jokes is all I got now," he says. You deny him a response, so he continues. "Can't tell you how much I'll miss taking a shit." He waits for a smirk, but you deny him this, too. "My starling, looka'me."

"It'll pain me."

"Aye, but do it all the same."

Eye contact has always hurt, ever since you were a boy– ah, no, you were never a boy– a child, then. Mum and Pa never believed you, that to look into a person's eyes was like looking into the sun, or like trying to heed a whisper while a hundred voices screamed. It was true, but they called you a fibber, a perjurer before God, and they caned you. Now, shame and revulsion are the greater reasons not to look into that box, even if it holds your whole world.

As if reading your mind, he goes on, "I want to see my beloved, if that you still are. Aye, I know, the hands you fasted to your own are probably ash on some pyre in Knothollow. But I'm still here."

To Hell with his jokes. You look at him.

It's a pistol-box his head is in, and it faces frontward as you left it. But his head has… he has… hopped, or something, to face you. Your gaze dances about his face, anywhere besides his attention. Same mop of red curls. Same full lips–blue now. Same long scar on his temple that draws an onlooker's attention to his own. But not *your* dodging glances, of course.

"Faithlost," you curse, and find his eyes. They're as they have been for the last week, since his execution, and then his being brought back. Glassy blue irises, always like he's drunk or about to cry. But the pupils, all four, well those're newer.

When you did what you did to bring him back, his pupils split from top to bottom, leaving them looking like hourglasses. Days later, when he tapped into the same forbidden magic to conjure a moon-globe for you and the horses to see by—two horses back then—the pupils split fully. Now they're two black globs drifting about in each eyeball. He said he can see fine, but it defies your studies of anatomy. You wish you could trust without understanding the thing yourself.

"Well? What do you see when you looka'me?" he asks.

"Nothing's changed," you answer, knowing he was asking something more tender than *how are my demon eyes?* Hell, maybe you were answering the question he was really asking. Or maybe, as usual, you were doing what's easy, not what's hard. Not what's soft. What does it matter?

He clears his throat, like he always did...*does* before beginning a jape.

"Aye, nothing has changed. Just a chopped head that's still talking, married to a witch more determined to be miserable than to live. Just your average pair of travelers, really."

"Warlock."

"Nuuh?"

"Don't, 'nuuh' it sounds feebleminded." That's Mum's favorite line. You go on. "A witch who's a man is called a warlock. I'm a man. As you might remember."

"Of course, my starling," he pleads, "'Twas the word, warlock, that's new to me, not..."

"...not?"

"Not you. It's a man I fell for, and a man I married, and a

man I love."

"Oh. Good."

"Please–"

His begging revolts you. "We should keep quiet. Boggits about."

"Piss off and shut up, you mean to say."

"If that's the meaning you take."

"It's the one you gave. I've me limits as well, even if you could punt me into the woods and be done with me."

He waits for you to say you never would. A third time, you deny him. He swallows it.

A time later, he begins the melancholy song from that tavern, the first night you laid eyes.

"My lover's like the ocean, tra la, tra loo, tra lye.

He takes my glee, gives misery, but without him, I'd die.

My lover's like a tempest, tra la, tra lee, tra lye.

His wrath and scorn are a mighty storm, but oh his rain gives life."

"S'horrible, that song. The lover is a monster. He breeds fear and reliance, not…not love.

He's a vampire, as sure as the one lives in Castle Graven."

"Anyone who's loved isn't a monster. Less'n he chooses to be."

"Aye, my misery's all my fault, " you say.

"If that's the meaning you take."

"It's the one you…" But you won't let him have even this small thing. What would you have left?

He says, "We were never monsters for loving."

You almost snort your contempt, lend some viciousness,

swat away his affection, but you stop yourself in time. Ah, so there is a limit to your cruelty. You try to stopper the tears inside your head.

"Twil ache later if you keep em in," he says, on cue.

Damn him for seeing you. Damn him for calling your bluff, for not giving up, and damn, damn, *damn* him for choosing you that first night, every dawn since. If he'd picked someone else to slump down next to at the bar, someone else with whom to trade coded innuendo, harmless lies, and dangerous truths.

You stop the wagon. The horse chuffs and steam rises from her back. You cry. After some time, you clean yourself up.

"Dying and surviving are on the same side of the great river, dear heart. Living, really living, is on the other side," he says.

"Which drunken tavern philosopher came up with that?"

"Me brain did just now."

"Shite it did."

"It did! Brain's about all I've got left, after all. Maybe I'm cultivating a genius for maudlin wank."

A branch snaps. The horse startles, looks around.

"Boggits," you whisper, sharp.

"Aye, aye, enough cowcrap from old dee-cap."

"Nay, truly. Boggits. At least six. God."

"Don't think God's our man anymore, love. Reckon we're in with the other fellow now."

"You said we weren't monsters."

"I said, 'less'n we wants to be.'"

He grins, looking into the forest, singing a protection

spell. Silence, until, in front of you, the iron spike holding the horse's yoke to the wagon-shaft scrapes its way out, pulled by an invisible hand. You and your husband watch it, awestruck. When it clears the socket, the yoke's shaft slaps loudly into the mud, and the panicking horse bolts. You're stranded.

"Can a boggit do that?" he asks.

"Nay. A hag is about. In this wood, perchance even Black Annis herself." From your satchel, you grab the tome on which your devil's pact was sealed and feel its pulse beating. The book wakes and begins its usual sobbing, leaking wet melancholy onto your hand. You hop into the mud, turn to him. "Stay. And mind your magic. Do *not* reach for something bigger than what you can tame."

They charge under blinding lightning. Sinewy, mold-green muscles, bald heads and needle- filled mouths. Anyone else could recover quickly from the flash. But not you, so at the mercy of sudden light and sound. You need time you don't have. Thunder silences your horse's scream.

Two senses gone, now, and you need them all.

Rage. Fear. You can use these for magic, but it will cost you.

You open the tome, though you memorized every word when you first read this miserable, self-pitying book at the bottom of that catacomb. You read it as an Inquisitrix, of course, to better know where darkness hides, and how better to destroy it. You couldn't help memorizing the horrid spells: *Soul Bleed*, *Transform*, and the worst of all, simply called, *Again*. You feigned ignorance until your church, your everything, caught you and him together, groaning along with

the creaking leather that held the oiled wood between your legs and into him.

The whole town cheered when they took his head as the wages of your salvation. They did not let you take the *contraption* off to watch it. So, you took the book, broke ground in the graveyard, and stole any hope of deliverance his soul may have had. You said the words, took his head—squalling like a babe, howling from sights none should see—and you ran.

But now, you speak other damned words, and fleshy horns rip through each temple, and a third awakens between your legs.

If they call you demon, so shall you be.

You hold your free hand forward, palm up, and feel a distant tug, like a fish nibbling bait.

Twist. The boggit crunches sideways, like wet cloth being wrung. Dead. But the other three are upon you before you can wring them. A claw rakes through your leathers, leaving a burning gash in your side.

Blinded, deafened, and now flooded with pain, the magick's purple hue cleanses to holly-berry red. You'll lose blood, but gain time, and time is dearer. You yell the words, and the voices of a million damned join your own, balling in your mouth like hot hair. The boggits fly backward. One is incinerated. Another breaks apart against a tree, and the last flees into the forest, smoldering and keening.

When your sight half-returns, lazy and drunken, you see that you've blown your husband's box and head off the side of the carriage and jump into the mud. Your whip-thick tail springs free of the back of your belt. You flail, still not used

to how your knees bend backward once the magick has you. You reach him and cradle his skull to your chest, putting out burning hair.

"Warn me, next time you explode, will you?" he says.

"Mmm. Mmmnnn…" Words have abandoned you. "Gnnnaaaaa. Yep–hmm."

Your horse screams like a woman, and your husband conjures light for you to see by. You wish he hadn't.

The horse floats ten feet above the mud, spinning like it's on a cooking spit, but fast, too fast, and kicking. Its skin is pulled off in one long ribbon, string off a dropped spool. That grim thread is woven into a lattice of gore, hovering by the edge of the treeline. Behind it dances a naked crone, dugs and gut splashing as she guides the living meat into her foul tapestry.

"Tis her," you say with dread, then, "we go."

His head turns in your hands, looking back at the cart. "But the books! The stamps, icons, and pedigrees! Your confirmation papers! Without them, we can't prove we're more than robbers, vagrants!"

"Should they?"

He closes his eyes. You retrieve your husband's box, hoist up your trousers, and run. As you pass the horse, stripped of flesh but somehow, awfully alive, you toss another wringing spell, snapping its neck. On the other side, Black Annis clothes herself from the skein of sinew she pulled from your horse, laughing, screaming. It covers her and squeezes tight. You turn his face to your chest and press on, knowing not to look back. Normal eyes make you squirm–looking at hers

would drive you—

But you *do* look back.

Weak.

She is young, now, and clothed in green finery. Her hair, once grey, have become ebon feathers, defying the storm. Her face, once long, coarse, and cruel, is now a statue, too beautiful to be real. Her flesh, once a mottled scab, is now firm, full, fat, pure dough under proof. She winks at you. Her voice thrusts into your mind.

"I see you, creature. And I know you. I know I'm not what you lust for. But the men of the world? The *real* men? They'll wage wars for just a taste. You have magic in your own little box there. Would you throw it all away out of pride?"

Sobbing, you hold him close. She grins, walks away, then climbs, cackling, into your cart to rummage. Her words burn, but there's power in surviving them.

Hours of walking later, he says, "Enough! Stop it!" and you realize you had been saying,

"Sorry, sorry, sorry—I'm sorry, *sorry*, so sorry, I'm sorry," for ages.

Hours later still, maybe a day, your hands ache and bleed from carrying the box with its sharp corners and no handle. Your horns and foul gift have retreated. Ahead, a stone bridge spanning a roaring waterfall. Beyond, you see a town behind a tall stockade. Safety. Maybe.

Along the road to the bridge, bodies hang from trees. They wear signs scrawled with their crimes. Your boggit wounds burn, surely infected, but you won't turn boggit

yourself. Your blood carries a stronger poison. Small mercies.

"I can't read the signs. What do they say? Do they say, 'witch?' or 'deviant?' 'Murderer?'"

His earnestness fills you with contempt.

"It's fine," you say, "they say nothing. Nothing at all."

You put your husband's head back in the box, close it, and fasten the lock. Maybe he protests, maybe he doesn't. You can't hear anything over the churn of the waterfall. You pause on the cold stone bridge and place the box on the low wall. You listen to the crashing water, and your headache finally breaks.

You push the box off and turn away before it hits the roil.

You tuck your tail back into your belt and arrange your hair like you used to before. You pound the stockade door with both bloody hands, finally, *finally*, free of the burden they carried for so long. Those same hands undo the top button of your tunic, and suddenly it is not *your tunic* but *her blouse*. Your hands, no, *her* hands, undo another button. A third for luck.

Good girl.

Mercifully, a man opens the door's small sliding window. He sees a bawling, bedraggled, desperate damsel. His favorite. She is looking him right in the eyes.

The gates open. She is safe.

LIKE NO BLOOD

ADRIAN SPETH

Thump.

Thump-shiver-twitch–

Thump-shiver-twitch-click-shiver-crack-twitch–

I have something in my hands. I wouldn't call it a gift, but christening it a curse would sound like whining to just about anyone else.

When I was eight years old, I lived with my dad out by the state highway. It was two lanes, the only road near the house. Speed limit was sixty, but you'd catch trucks doing eighty, and anything hit at that speed was as good as dead. That summer, I would walk along that highway, sometimes a mile in either direction, chipping at the cracked asphalt with the toe of my sneaker. This was before I knew I liked boys but after I'd learned I liked animals, and somewhere in between the two I picked up an unflinching fascination with dead things. The road obliged my interest–the tires of the passing cars and trucks left plenty behind to study.

Two weeks after I'd blown out eight red candles, wishing for something hazy and hardly remembered, someone's tires caught a jackrabbit. I found it stone dead within sight of my dad's house, its gray fur dyed crimson and purple, flank twisted and punctured by gravel and slick white bone. One of its ears was shredded and limp, but the other had inexplicably escaped harm.

The inside was still a soft pink, and delicate, like it might still be able to hear me. I wondered briefly if it listened to the rest of its body die. If the sound was still trapped in there somewhere, like a pearl in an oyster.

It hadn't been dead long, and even in the July heat, there were only two or three flies buzzing around. The blood didn't bother me. It never bothered me much with roadkill, not like the way it would coming out of a human body. I studied the rabbit for a while, barely noticing the cars still whizzing past.

And I picked it up.

I don't know why I did it. I'd been told you could catch a million things from the live vermin around those parts, never mind what was crushed and rotting out on the highway. But I picked it up. It was stiff, already bloating, and it made a sound as I peeled it away from the asphalt that reminded me of velcro. I stood there with it, sort of cradling it against my chest, that one long and perfect ear hanging listlessly against my shirt. The air was hot. The flies buzzed.

My hands itched.

Thump–

Thump-shiver–

Thump-shiver-twitch—

It shuddered to life against me.

I was so shocked I dropped it. The rabbit landed back with a *thump* on the asphalt it had just been smeared across, writhing to regain its feet. Then it just sat there, twitchy, looking up at me. Its hind leg *thumped* again against the road as the bone twisted and righted itself. I could still see bits of shattered bone in its fur, now patched over like an old rug. The torn-up ear hung limply, but as I watched it spasmed, stitched, and shot upright. Just a regular jackrabbit, flesh and bone and breathing.

We stared at each other, and I knew by the shiver and twitch of its skin that whatever I'd done, it wasn't done right. That's the curse of it, I think. To hold life in your hands and find it *wrong*. Men have fought wars and killed millions for the right to that decision and the universe just decided to hand it on down to me.

I didn't want it. I turned and ran. I scrubbed my hands that night until they were cracked and raw, but the *thump-twitch* of the rabbit remained.

The rabbit might have been the first, but it wouldn't be the last. No matter how I did it, no matter how deserved the second chance, none of them were ever quite right.

Rory wasn't a rabbit. Rory was a man as much as I was, different as night and day but both of us men. He grew his hair long; I panicked if mine so much as tickled my neck. He gave himself weekly shots while I rubbed gel into my shoulders. The texture of honey I used to eat by the spoonful as a kid could send him into a panic attack. I'd never been fond of change,

but the two of us changed together, and he changed the way I felt love.

Rory could sing. Over the course of our three-year relationship, I listened to his voice drop from alto to baritone. He wasn't afraid of needles and always laughed at me when I couldn't watch him do his shot in the bathroom.

"There's, like, no blood this time," he called to me once.

"Like no blood or *actually* no blood?" I called back.

"Like no blood."

"That's too much blood."

I wasn't exaggerating. Even the bead of it the needle left behind was enough to send the room spinning. It wasn't the blood, not really; it was the nature of it. Coming from a living thing instead of caked in the dead grass by the highway. Blood outside a living body is a life gone slightly wrong.

I don't like to think about how it happened the first time. I came home late—a shift in routine that made my skin crawl but I could do nothing about. The apartment was quiet, the lights in the front room on but illuminating nothing. I hung my jacket up and put my bag on the couch like I did every night.

"Rory?" I called. I received no answer. Faintly, I could hear the water in the bathtub running. He never showered this late. My heart skipped and shivered. A muscle just below my left eye twitched. I crept for the bathroom door, listening for any clue as to what had thrown off the nature of things so badly. There was another sound now, soft and familiar under the running water, a strange buzzing I couldn't quite place.

I knocked. "Rory. Are you okay?"

No response.

I eased the door open and slipped inside. He hadn't locked it; he would forget to lock the front door if I weren't around. My eyes fell on the sink first. I saw his electric razor, still buzzing harshly against the porcelain sink. I reached out and switched it off. In the corner of my vision, I could see the bathtub. Taking another shuffling step into the bathroom, eyes still glued on his razor balanced on the edge of the sink, my shoes splashed in water overflowing from the tub. My heart raced. My eyes slid from the corner of the sink to the floor and slowly over to where Rory floated, half in and half out, folded over the side of the bathtub where he had fallen.

The blood in the water was like nothing I'd ever seen.

He must have slipped. Slipped or fainted, I would never know, but there was still a sick spatter of crimson where his head struck the acrylic rim of the tub. *Thump*. I slipped on my way to him, my hands pleading and frantic on his shoulders, hauling him out of the tub, begging him to breathe. *Thump-shiver.* He slumped in my arms, water streaming from his hair and trickling out of his mouth. The back of his head felt wrong. *Thump-shiver-crack.* Fragmented. Puzzle pieces that didn't fit together right anymore. There was no point in CPR—I was far too late.

I propped him up against the tub and watched his head loll back, his hair streaming out behind him in the water. I sat next to him and cried, long and hard, knowing what was proper to do but not wanting to do it. Call the police. Call his parents. Start preparing for a life forever without him. Between hiccuping sobs, something rose fast and unavoidable in my throat, and I scrambled for the toilet. As I retched, I remembered that day I

spent on the highway just past eight years old. The jackrabbit and the twitchy startup of a silenced heart. I wiped my mouth on the back of my hand, still shaking. I looked over at Rory, still lying slumped against the bathtub, his head back in the water and his throat exposed to the air.

Thump-shiver-twitch-shiver–

It took all my energy to get him back in the tub. A waterlogged corpse is heavier than you think and I was still unsteady from crying, but I thought it best to begin in the exact place he died. Less room for error that way. Rory was dead weight in my arms. Blood oozed from his head as it rolled against the rim. The same blood stained my hands, and I wiped them furiously on my jeans until they felt raw and rushed and ready to work.

I placed one hand on Rory's chest and cradled his head with the other. His silence and his stillness were more than I could bear, so I pushed him beneath the surface before I could begin crying again. The air was humid. Above us, a fly buzzed, trapped in the harsh overhead light. My hands ached and itched.

Thump–

Thump-shiver–

Thump-shiver-twitch-click–

Rory surged up out of the water. I opened my eyes. He flailed, spilling water over the sides of the tub as he gasped for air. I dragged him out even as he jerked and thrashed, his limbs remembering life. When I let go, he scrambled backwards on all fours. His hair hung in his face, hiding his eyes.

"It's me," I said.

"I was dead," he choked out.

All I could do was repeat it. "It's me."

His skin shuddered, and he gasped like I'd rubbed my feet across carpet and shocked him. "You did this," he said, and then again, as if he were my mirror, "You did this."

"I love you." It was all I could think to say.

"What happened?"

"You fell," I told him.

He shook his head and winced. "More than that."

"Yes," I agreed, and then, "We can talk about it later. How do you feel?"

"Broken," he whispered. Something near the base of his skull cracked. He grunted.

"Better."

Jackrabbit on the highway. *Thump-shiver-twitch-snap* as the body remembered its purpose. Fur patched and plastered over a bag of broken bones.

We went to sleep together that night, side by side and rigid as the grave. His breath rattled. I held my own. When I touched him, I could feel only broken skin twisted around a delicate skeleton. Both our hollow heartbeats echoed in my ears.

I wish I could say the days passed easily. We talked, first about the fall and then about the jackrabbit, and finally about Rory's strange new chance at life. He seemed to take all of it as well as could be expected. He didn't say much about what it was like to be dead—he didn't really say much of anything. He went back to work, and then I did, and we tried to continue on with our lives.

The first thing I noticed was his laugh—rather, it was the *lack* of it that I noticed. He was silent at jokes that he used to find funny, and even the smile he'd offer up in place of it felt wrong, smeared across his face like a messy afterthought. When he *did* laugh, it echoed weirdly.

He seemed unbothered, but it gnawed at me with dull teeth.

From then on, it was easy to notice everything wrong. When you know someone better than the back of your hand, it's too easy to convince yourself you don't. Too easy to misremember a mole, or a freckle, or the timbre of a voice. The more I looked at Rory, the less I remembered him. The tighter I held him, the more foreign he felt. Like the rabbit, and all the things after the rabbit, he was wrong. I had done wrong and I had made him wrong.

My hands itched. My mind twitched. I did this, but maybe I could undo it. Like untying and retying a bow. A cycle of beginnings and ends.

I let a week pass. Two. In the middle of the third week, I told myself the longer I waited, the more he'd rot. That's all this was—a sort of waking decay. He did his shot Wednesday night, like always. That much never changed. I paced back and forth outside the bathroom until I thought he'd finished. He wanted to watch a movie afterwards. I had one picked out, but I prayed to whatever put the gift in my hands that I would meet him in the bathroom, not in our living room. I knew if he emerged—if he gave me a hug or kissed me or even laughed that weird new *shiver-clack* laugh of his—I wouldn't be able to do it. Even standing outside the bathroom, I was afraid I would lose myself to fear.

I knocked. "Finished?"

"Almost."

"Blood?"

"Not this time."

The room spun anyway. I clutched the doorknob for balance, watched my knuckles turn white and bloodless around it, and then eased the door open and slipped inside. He was running a bath, and sat on the edge of the tub in his binder and an old pair of sweatpants. I couldn't remember the last time I'd seen him wearing them, or the last time he hadn't bled at least a little.

I couldn't remember his smile ever making me feel so nauseous.

"Did it hurt?" I asked him.

"Not really," he said.

"It usually hurts, though."

"Not always."

"You usually bleed."

His voice was gentle. "Not always, love."

My hands twitched. Black asphalt and beating sun. Even in the harsh white bathroom light, Rory's eyes were as dark as road tar. "Have you tried singing again?" I asked.

He shrugged. "Earlier."

"And?"

"It'll come back." Still, he smiled up at me, and although his face twisted like a stranger's, he was as easy and unassuming as always. "You said it might take time."

"Yes," I said, and then again, "Yes, I did. But I—"

He wasn't looking at me. Stretched around to shut off the water, the muscles across his shoulders and back strained away from me. I shut the door. Locked it. The muffled *thump-click* of the door in its frame and the lock in its place made him turn back. His smile was quizzical now. "Sticking around?"

"I'm sorry," I took a step forward. My hands twitched again.

Rory's lips twitched in time. "For what?"

"This is my fault." Another step. Sneaker soles scraping against sticky gravel. The buzz of flies. The buzz of an electric razor. The buzz of my own blood in my ears. *Thump-shiver-twitch-crack-click–*

"But I can fix it," I continued. "Give me one more chance and I'll get you right."

"Get me…" His voice faded with his smile. "Hey. Let's talk, yeah? I'm okay, so let's just talk."

"You've changed." Another step. One more and I'd be able to reach him. I kept my hands at my sides. "You're not you. We both know it. If you give me one more chance I can fix it. I can make you sing again. I can put you right."

"You can't put me right." Rory stood up, body tense and wary like the jackrabbit's ears.

He made no move to attack me, no move to flee. He spoke very slowly. "I'm still me. You brought me back."

"You're different." I couldn't stop my words from shaking. "We always said we'd change together, but you're different without me now. I did something *wrong*–"

"Please calm down."

"We have to go back." One more step. Just one more.

"We were both in the past—"

"Cal."

"—and then I dragged you into the future and, and *something* got lost between the two—"

"Cal, please." He was scared now. I could almost hear the wild frenzy of his heartbeat.

"Nothing got lost. It's me. It's only me."

"No." I shook my head. "No, that's not true, but I promise you if you just trust me I can fix it."

"It doesn't work like that." He was trying to step around me, leaning one way and then the other, ready to spring. I moved with him and he froze. He tried again. "Time doesn't run backward. It doesn't even run *forward*, every second just exists until another one replaces it. We're entirely in the present. Maybe you want me how I used to be, but maybe I can never be that. That's *okay*." His voice quivered in his throat. *Twitch-shiver.*

"Okay," I echoed.

He nodded. "It's okay."

"It's okay." I took a deep breath. "No blood. It's okay."

"Wait—"

I lunged for him. The force sent both of us crashing into the bathtub. Water sloshed and spilled over the sides as we wrestled. Rory twisted and thrashed and managed to roll over on top of me, but I hooked my arm around his neck and dragged him back, locking him against my chest. I slid down into the tub, submerging us up to my neck. He sputtered and coughed and spit water but I just slid lower, keeping my chin above the surface and keeping him just below it. His hands scrabbled at the sides of the tub and reached back for my face, but I held him close and I whispered, "It's okay. No blood. It's okay." I felt his body straining for the life it had already been once denied. His heartbeat *thumped* wildly against my forearm.

I remembered bloody fur under a July sun and life gone wrong under my hands and a stranger in a body I used to know so well, and then with one final shudder I was alone and alive in the bathtub.

I sat up slowly, bringing him with me. He made no noise or movement when he broke the surface. His head lolled forward, his chin nuzzling against my arm, as limp as the one perfect ear of the jackrabbit. He felt so peaceful. He wasn't bleeding. Not like the rabbit, not like before. No sign of life gone wrong. No sign of life at all.

I kissed the top of his head and closed my eyes. We'd watch a movie when he came back.

I'd already picked one out. He'd laugh. It would sound good in his chest.

The water was hot. Above us, around the light, a fly buzzed. My hands itched.

Thump.

Thump-shiver-twitch–

Thump-shiver-twitch-click-shiver-crack-twitch–

THESE THIRTEEN SIMPLE TRICKS WILL END YOUR SLEEP HALLUCINATIONS FOR GOOD

CATHERINE FORREST

I.

If you wake with your heart racing, and the bald man with hooded eyes leans over you, simply blink. He will vanish. This is guaranteed to work.

II.

When you find yourself awake in the dark with an uneasy feeling, check the far corner of the room behind the chair heaped with semi-dirty clothes. You may spot a shadow with no logical source; that is likely the cause of your unease. Spend three eternities questioning whether the shadow was there yesterday. Midway through the third eternity, nod off.

III.

If the bald man is standing at the bay window with his profile limned by moonlight, and if he notices you noticing him, and if he folds his hands together against the belly of his lab coat, stare at him unblinking until he disintegrates.

IV.

When you wake and he is in the room again, but you're tired and have work tomorrow, roll over and go back to sleep. He will no longer be there in the morning.

V.

Say, in the calmest and firmest voice you can manage, "I know you're there." Wait for a response—stay awake as long as you can. Eventually you will fall asleep and wake to the chirping of birds.

VI.

Grab the nearest object, your cell phone, and throw it at the bald man and his associate, the clipboard lady. You will not hit them—don't be alarmed! This is likely due to grogginess.

Nothing is wrong with your aim. The clatter of your device against the wall between them will be very loud in your quiet bedroom. In the morning your phone will be on the nightstand, plugged in.

VII.

Set a trap.

Step 1. Acquire a bucket. The dollar store has one for children to play with at the beach. That will work fine.

Step 2. Fill your bucket with broken glass.

Step 3. Open your bedroom door approximately half as wide as the diameter of the bucket.

Step 4. Climb on the dresser and balance the bucket on the open door such that the bucket is slightly unbalanced—not unlike yourself!—and leaning against the lintel.

Note: While broken glass is best, you could fill the bucket with razor blades or steak knives if there is no glass on hand. Be creative!

Although the bald man comes at night, the bucket will be undisturbed in the morning.

Climb on the dresser again. Disarm the trap.

VIII.

Lie still with your eyes closed and keep your breathing even; give every impression you are still asleep. Try to hear what they are saying behind the faceplates of their hazmat suits. Try to remember so you can write it down tomorrow.

IX.

Advanced tip—for experienced lucid dreamers only!

Leave your body. Drift around the ceiling until you have confirmed the bald man and his colleagues are watching your flesh and have not noticed your astral projection. With their attention otherwise focused, circle around behind them. Try to see what the lady is writing on her clipboard.

X.

Communication is key: Ask the bald man what he wants with you. He will tilt his head eighteen degrees to the right and

pull his brows together. Then his lips will move and noise will come out, but it will not sound like speech. The noise comes from very far away.

It can't, though. Your bedroom is twelve feet, five inches square and he is definitely in the room.

XI.

Ask yourself whether this might be a sleep study: Perhaps a new type you haven't heard of in which the subject of the study is kept unaware for important scientific reasons. Tell yourself this will all end soon, probably with a prescription for a CPAP machine. Be convincing.

XII.

Attack: This method requires some advance preparation. You will need several years of kenpo lessons from the place over on High Point, and you will need to make sure the daytime associates of your night visitors do not see you going to and from. If you don't have years, which you don't, then in lieu of kenpo you can take the two-week self-defense course at the community center.

Choose your moment: Wait for the bald man to come alone. When he leans over to take your pulse at the carotid, go for his eyeballs with your thumbs. Unfortunately, your hands will get tangled in the sheets. You will not have the opportunity again.

XIII.

When all else fails, accept the things you cannot change. When the needle goes in, maybe just let it.

A DREAM SO SWEET

CHRIS NELSON

Something that looked very much like a man fled across the wasteland, knowing the solution to a riddle. For many days a linguist had pursued the riddle's answer through the thunder-blasted desolation of this forsaken place, following the burning footprints the man-shaped thing left behind it in the sand.

The thing had a way of slipping from view like water slips through fingers, so he had resorted to tracking it in infrared.

The linguist halted suddenly upon something on the ground and looked up, squinting into the distance. Already the crumbling towers of a ruined city rose from the far horizon. And there, only just visible against the undulating heat, was the tiny man-shaped silhouette of the thing. He was gaining on it.

He looked back down to the deterrent his quarry had left in its wake.

There, scrawled large and hastily in the sand, was:

AGONY IS THE ANSWER TOO!

The Solipsist

Excerpt from Act I, Scene 3:

[REUBEN lies in bed. Enter SILAS, carrying a bucket.]

SILAS: I just got everything. Nutmeg, turmeric, cumin—I couldn't remember which one it was. And a journal, uh, the melatonin, and a list of websites. There's a ton online, most of it shit. I forgot the pen.

REUBEN: What...oh.

SILAS: [He sits at the foot of the bed.] I wanna try to help, if I can.

REUBEN: You changed your mind.

SILAS: I was thinking about-trying to figure out the farthest I've ever been from Lana, and I decided it was probably that time she went abroad, back in college, before we even met. There was a whole planet separating us for like, almost a year. And— that started to make me feel light-headed, man. I thought, if she were one whole world away from me now, I would be willing to

walk all the fucking way around the globe to get to her. I thought, even if she were, I don't know, in a spaceship travelling at—at like, extraluminary velocity, away from the Earth out into outer space, I could *try* to get another ship built, I could *try* to follow her, even if I had to spend the rest of my life trying. I could *do* something. We'd still be in the same *universe*. …And then I started to think about… how… [He begins to cry.]

REUBEN: Silas.

SILAS: I started to think about how far *you* are from *your* person. You're *more* than lightyears from being able to hold him, from being able to tell him… it clicked for me.

REUBEN: Thank you, Silas.

SILAS: Why am *I* the one crying?

REUBEN: The flesh is weak, dude.

SILAS: I'll help you. You'll see him again.

REUBEN: [He examines a bottle of nutmeg.] What am I supposed to do? Just consume this raw?

SILAS: I do not fucking know, man.

"As Many Words as Grains of Sand" was how the linguist translated his own name into English once he learned the necessary words. His wife, whose name he rendered as "In

Silk Bedight," was a spinner of shrouds. She had been dyeing a wedding shroud two gorgeous shades of midnight blue on the morning her husband came to her with the news.

They had finally found a signal, he told her. He explained where it was and what it probably represented, and after a moment she realized that he wanted to go. She blinked her many eyes, tapping one of her bladelike forelimbs upon her husband's hard carapace in a gesture of affection. She said that she did not wish to go—that she was afraid, that she would miss their children; but she had always followed him, and she would not fail to follow him now. Did he really want to go?

He replied that, yes, he wanted to very much: this was not only an opportunity to collect new words, it was an opportunity to collect *alien* words, the stuff of completely different minds. So, in the end, they left their four young children in the care of a trusted wet nurse and set out in a ship towards the source of the signal.

What they found there was a library, full of books and floating in space.

And among those books was an essay on a play entitled *The Solipsist*.

"In early 2024, Benjamin Euwer published his debut three-act drama about a man named Reuben and his efforts to achieve a lucid dream after the death of an unnamed husband. It is in this play that Euwer establishes his Theory of Goodness and its relationship to human consciousness. Despite several questions of plot left unanswered,

moments of impenetrable density, and an ending that G. W. Morgan criticizes as 'conspicuously highbrow,' the ideas presented in The Solipsist were, at the very least, unprecedented at the time of their introduction."

For a long time As Many Words as Grains of Sand haunted the library, clambering from shelf to shelf and puzzling with several gangly limbs over book after book. At first he let his dozens of eyes float over the enigmatic texts, gleaning patterns and deducing the meanings of words from their forms and contexts. He was significantly more intelligent than the beings who had created the library, and soon he had learned most of the words of their language and how to combine them into sentences.

He learned the word "librarian" and applied it to those who had constructed the library. He found pictures of the librarians and was surprised at what sheer aliens they were. Although their two races shared a basic bilateral symmetry, comparable metabolisms, and a similar set of sensory organs clustered in a head, they differed radically in other respects. Indeed, the linguist and his wife resembled something the librarians called "spiders," at least superficially, more than they resembled the librarians themselves—although these spiders were, evidently, much smaller creatures, and they did not have a language.

"Spider," As Many Words as Grains of Sand said in English, savoring the taste and feel of the word. "Cognate with the verb *to spin*, I would guess." In Silk Bedight, meanwhile, spun her shrouds and practiced idioms with her husband.

Then he found the book of essays. It was a very dense text, and it took him a long time to disentangle its threads. The more he deciphered, the more mysterious it all became: the librarians underwent a kind of torpor once a night, and had strange visions which they regarded as partly real and partly unreal.

One of the essays discussed a play in which a librarian attempted to have a special kind of vision. As Many Words as Grains of Sand became fascinated by the play within the essay—but, try as he might, he could not solve the riddle within the play.

"We have to know them," he told his wife.

She set her shroud gingerly aside and said: "I will follow you."

Another book in the library proved to be an atlas of the galactic vicinity, and the mathematical notation used was easily deduced; numbers, after all, are universal, even if words are not. The maps within were two-dimensional like the pages which held them, but by comparing two different maps from two different perspectives, the linguist and his wife were able to extrapolate the position of a planet labelled "ours." Then they wrote eight goodbye letters before jumping in their ship to the librarians' homeworld.

What As Many Words as Grains of Sand found there looked very much like a man, poking at a dying fire and babbling lunacies to itself in the wastes. But the thing was not a man, and when the linguist mentioned *The Solipsist*, it screamed in fright and vanished before his eyes.

A DREAM SO SWEET

The Solipsist

Excerpt from Act II, Scene 4:

DR. ALLUM: Silas must care about you a great deal.

REUBEN: Did he tell you why I agreed to come?

DR. ALLUM: Yes. I'd like to discuss the lucid dreaming with you.

REUBEN: You think I just need to stop *investing*, rewire pathways until I can achieve some quality of life again. I can't see things around the distortion of my own viewpoint, after all.

DR. ALLUM: [She sighs.] Perhaps conventionally. But I am a pragmatist, Reuben. It took me a long time to realize this, but the ends really do justify the means. Time is a funny thing. All that matters is how you feel.

REUBEN: What if I feel like life isn't worth living anymore?

DR. ALLUM: Then something must change.

REUBEN: You have no idea how worthless I feel.

DR. ALLUM: Then tell me. What do you miss most about him? Tell me something you still love about him.

REUBEN: It hurts so much when you say

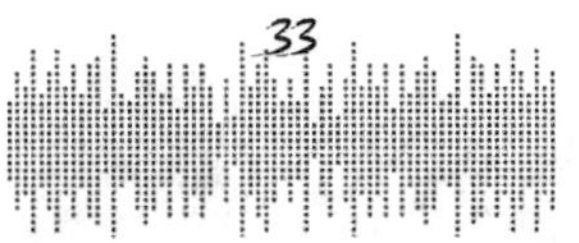

things like that, you *lunatic*.

DR. ALLUM: Silas told me I'd...have to *trick* you into feeling better. He said you needed, um, "the smartest therapist in Seattle." I truly think it would help if you could talk with me.

REUBEN: Talk with—with *you*? About *what*, about how we weren't even *supposed* to fall in love with each other, because our *parts* didn't correspond? About how it happened anyway, and now he's *dead*?

DR. ALLUM: I have no *idea* what it's like to feel like you're feeling right now, Reuben.

REUBEN: You want to know why I loved him? The moment I first knew?

DR. ALLUM: Yes. I really do.

[A pause.]

REUBEN: One time, when we first got married, we were lying in bed, talking about—about what we...liked. What we enjoyed sexually. And...and one of us said...

[Another pause.]

DR. ALLUM: Please take your time.

REUBEN: One of us said, "Your pleasure is sixty percent of my pleasure."

[An even longer pause.]

DR. ALLUM: That's a lovely sentiment, Reuben. Thank you for sharing that with me.

REUBEN: I don't remember which one of

us said it. I can't remember if it even happened, or if it was something I dreamed.

As Many Words as Grains of Sand hypothesized the man-shaped thing's skin contained dedicated chromatophores that mimicked the colors of the environment. But the thing could not conceal its heat signature, which he followed to a city that had ages ago been Cairo.

He was alone. His wife refused to risk orphaning their children and did not follow him down to the planet.

Now the linguist crept through the wreckage of the city, listening for signs of the man-shaped thing. "Hello!" he called in English and Hadza and Cantonese.

He listened closely to the echoes that resounded all around him, but could not discern the shape of the thing within. "Please, I only want to talk to—"

His six keen ears twitched: a spill of tiny pebbles far away. He sprang after the sound, skittering over walls and under arches. The man-shaped glimpse fled; but, triangulating echoes and flickers, the linguist managed to corral the thing, drive it down a bridge, broken in the middle of its span, and corner it there. The thing stumbled, sprawling to the very edge, its chromatophores darkening.

"I mean you no harm!" he declared in English and then in Arabic as he advanced. "I only want to discuss the play with you!"

The thing's eyes flitted up toward the sky. As Many Words as Grains of Sand followed its eyeline to the shining sun, now almost directly overhead.

Looking back down to the man-shaped thing, he said: "If

you don't want—"

Suddenly the thing's skin snapped from pitch black to brilliant, blinding white. The linguist was stunned by the reflected sunburst and flinched, scuttling backwards. The shimmering man-shape took advantage by seizing a nearby piece of rubble and hurling it at him, but he parried the projectile and scrambled after the thing as it slipped past and out of sight.

The man-shaped thing, invisible now against the slate-gray metal of the surrounding ruins, sped through crevices, thoroughfares and rifts, eluding the shadow of its giant echolocating pursuer. Then there were two shadows flying over the ruins. The thing skidded just short of a wide gossamer web gleaming in the sunlight, strung taut from one crumbling pylon to another. Having evaded the web, it spun around to find itself face to face with a second gigantic spider, different from the one that had tracked it across the desert. Chromatophores flooded its skin, but calculating camouflage so quickly against two opponents' viewpoints took time, and before the thing could disappear the linguist snatched it up and wound it in an inescapably strict cocoon.

As Many Words as Grains of Sand clutched the cocoon tightly to his thorax, breathing heavily. He looked at his wife. "You came," he said in their native language. "You followed me."

Two-thirds of her primary eyes glanced at the swaddled figure of the man- shaped thing struggling within silken bonds. "You needed me to, it seems," she said in a language, dead a thousand years, which provided a suffix indicating

knowledge formerly possessed by the speaker alone, now shared with the listener.

"Crucially, the playwright distinguishes subjective experience per se from other brain-produced phenomena such as intelligence, theory of mind, memory, or even language. He contends that intelligence, for example, (that is, the capacity to formulate patterns and manipulate data) does not necessarily imply consciousness in the narrower sense. This allows for the possibility of so-called 'philosophical zombies': entities which appear normal but lack conscious experience, qualia, or sentience."

A pale spotlight shone down upon the man-shaped thing, now a dark gray, shackled to the center of the dim chamber. Two enormous spider-shapes lurked in the shadows, breathing silently.

Slowly, the thing looked up at them. It grinned. "There is no word that answers the riddle."

The linguist and his wife exchanged glances with some of their eyes before looking back.

"Is there not?" asked As Many Words as Grains of Sand. "But... even if there is not a word *yet*, could we not *coin* a word to represent the concept?"

"If there is no word for it, then the concept must not be important to the speakers," In Silk Bedight suggested.

The thing tilted its head to one side, skin slowly growing darker. "You're female, aren't you?" it said, staring at In Silk Bedight. "You're the female, and he's the male. That's why

he's obsessed with metaphysics while *you're* worried about staying alive. The gender that devotes more resources towards reproduction is doomed to be the more pragmatic sex." The thing chuckled and shook its head. "They were the exact same way."

"*Who* were the same?" As Many Words as Grains of Sand asked. "Your species? What happened to them? Where did they go?"

The man-shaped thing grinned hideously. Pink splotches began blossoming all over its black skin like an evil blush. "*My* species? Oh, I'm not a species, my friends. I'm a lonely little toy they built right before they died."

In Silk Bedight crouched. "A...toy?"

"They *built* you," the linguist realized. "But—in their image, which means you must understand the riddle as *they* once did!"

For a moment the man-shaped thing stared at them, dumbfounded.

"*WHAT!?*" it shouted. "You take the bitter with the sweet! Half the riddle's answer is *intrinsically* bad!"

"You said there was no word for the riddle's answer," As Many Words as Grains of Sand said. "Please—try to use your words in a way we can understand."

"Words?" the thing spat. "You want *words*? Fine! *Counterintuitively.* Banana! Rime-encrusted ziggurats! Here are some words, Spider-Man: *we* are sapient, but *they* were *sentient.* Is it my fault that the words get conflated? What if you're not *self*-aware, but aware of other things—is *that* conscious? Do computers have free will? Do gerbils think

that they are *anything*? This sentence is a lie! The *previous* sentence is a lie! THE *PREVIOUS—*"

"Stop it." As Many Words as Grains of Sand clacked a forelimb against the hard floor. "You are not even *trying* to communicate. You are not respecting the words you use. We cannot solve the riddle in Euwer's play unless--"

"You *stupid* fucking aliens!" the thing screamed. "Did you not *read* the play?! We *cannot* solve the riddle, because we are *asleep*! And if we wake up we will find ourselves in *HELL*!"

The Solipsist

Excerpt from Act III, Scene 4:

SILAS: You saw him.

REUBEN: I didn't do anything.

SILAS: Reuben, I—I don't know what to say! What finally did the trick? Did you see a dream sign?

REUBEN: I was talking…to you actually, about—well, about lucid dreaming. I guess because I spend so much time thinking about it in real life. You asked if I had seen a dream sign. And…I suddenly realized that I was dreaming, and soon I was able to control my dream.

SILAS: Reuben, that's… Why are you—

REUBEN: When he looked up at me, he said… "Reuben, I have missed you to pieces"—

[Reuben begins to cry. Silas embraces him.]

SILAS: It's okay. Let it out, man.

REUBEN: I was so happy. And then, just for a moment, right after I woke up, I hadn't yet remembered that he was…gone. And it was nothing short of…euphoria, to feel okay again. Then I remembered. He's dead. This is the nightmare I have to live inside until the day *I* die.

In Silk Bedight whispered that the man-shaped thing in front of them was insane, that it was reading Benjamin Euwer's damnable play which had driven it to madness, and if they pursued this forbidden knowledge they risked losing their own sanity.

As Many Words as Grains of Sand turned to her. "Speak English," he said.

"Please. That's the only way we're going to understand what's going on. *Their* words express *their* thoughts."

In Silk Bedight blinked her rows of primary eyes in sequence, two by two by two: their version of a sigh. "You always had such a faith in words," she said.

"They're all we have." He turned back to their prisoner. "…And if we can solve the riddle, we can experience its answer. '*Dichromatic experience*' must mean that there were two, oh, *flavors* of—"

The thing glanced from her to him with a look of panic. Curling ribbons of blue and green and white streamed across its black surfaces. "IF YOU DO THIS—" it screamed, "—IF YOU

SOLVE THE RIDDLE, I'LL—I'LL—I'LL—I'LL *EAT YOUR BABIES!!*"

The thing's skin went dark like a snuffed candle.

In Silk Bedight glowered. "Do not say that," she said, her voice low and somehow cold.

The thing stared back at her, eyes bulging freakishly from their sockets. A thin, malevolent smile spread slowly across its face. "I'll *eat* them," it said, and licked its lips.

"Stop," In Silk Bedight warned, taking one long, ungainly gallop towards it.

The thing looked simultaneously giddy and horrified. "IF YOU SOLVE THE RIDDLE, YOUR EGGS WILL—WILL CURDLE IN THEIR *SACS!*" it shouted. "THEY'LL CURDLE, OH HOW THEY'LL *CURDLE*, BUT I'M STILL GONNA EAT THEM, AND THEN I'LL VOMIT THEM BACK UP!"

In Silk Bedight advanced upon the thing, chittering menacingly. "*Stop it,*" she hissed. "*Stop talking about my babies or their mother will KILL YOU.*"

Suddenly As Many Words as Grains of Sand realized the thing was *trying* to goad his wife. It would rather die than solve the riddle.

"*Wait—!*" the linguist cried. He moved to restrain his wife, but she pulled away.

The thing strained against its chains and shrieked: "*YOUR CHILDREN WILL SCREAM FOR THEIR MOTHER AS I—*"

In Silk Bedight lurched forward and used five of her limbs to tear the thing's head messily from its body. As Many Words as Grains of Sand inhaled as the head thudded upon the deck. Rainbow blood squirted from the severed neck of the thing as its body, still spasming, slouched to the floor.

"AAAAAAAAH!" In Silk Bedight roared, grabbing hold of the ragged body and smashing it against the wall.

As Many Words as Grains of Sand looked down at the disembodied head with heinous triumph in its unseeing eyes. Then he looked to his wife, saying nothing. He wondered what the thing had feared could be worse than dying.

Breathing heavily, In Silk Bedight turned to face her husband. "Enough," she said. "Now we return home."

"Perhaps the clearest articulation of Euwer's Theory of Goodness can be found in the 'riddle' posed by Reuben in the first scene of Act II:

REUBEN: He's going to be real to me. Isn't that what matters?

SILAS: What difference does it make? If he's dead, then in what sense will he be real?

REUBEN: What does dying take from life that dreaming gives to sleep? What is it beholders hold, if not this dichromatic experience? What's the only thing we ever know but never can explain?

"Euwer's reasons for employing a roundabout description in lieu of a specific term are twofold: First, the playwright avoids conflating terminology that he considers fundamentally distinct, such as intelligence or the capacity for language. Second, the form of a riddle imbues an otherwise mundane phenomenon with a sense of the uncanny, forcing the reader to reconsider

it afresh. The concept Euwer circumlocutes using three questions is compatible only with a narrow formulation of consciousness: one consistent with the so-called 'hard problem.' All three questions, then, can be answered with a single concept—one that might be glossed as 'conscious, subjective experience of qualia.'"

As Many Words as Grains of Sand pondered the head, created in the image of a species of dreamers, which he held aloft in front of all his eyes. The head, drained of its chameleon blood, was now a noncommittal dull color. Eyes bulged vacantly, a pale tongue lolled in a still-grinning mouth. He drew the head in towards himself, tilting it slowly in the dim light, as though some new facet might reveal something of the minds of its unfathomable creators.

"To see, or not to see," the linguist whispered. "That is the answer."

In Silk Bedight loomed in a nearby portal, tapping one of her forelimbs absently against its metallic rim. "I'm sorry that you did not find what you were looking for."

As Many Words as Grains of Sand recognized her use of English as a gesture of reconciliation. He turned to her and chittered softly. "It doesn't matter," he said, feigning contentment. "I am ready to go home."

In Silk Bedight had been married to her husband long enough to know that he was lying. "Well," she said nonetheless, "you may not have solved the riddle, but--" She hesitated, then lapsed into their native language to utter a sequence of five words which corresponded, albeit imperfectly, to the

notion expressed by the English sentence "I love you."

She used the absolute evidentiality marker. Then she left.

He turned his attention back to the head.

"What does dying take from life...that dreaming gives to sleep?" he muttered. "What am I *missing*?"

He did not know the answer to the questions he posed. There was no way he could have; whatever the answer to the riddle was, his brain didn't generate any of it.

SURVIVE LOT 666

CAROLINE HUNG

Good evening, it's Meifong speaking. Welcome to our *SURVIVE* series–the widely-popular and award-winning reality show where I, your talented host, venture far outside human civilization to enter the urban jungles of Metro Manila.

On tonight's episode, we're challenging the infamous LOT 666 and its dangerous trails, numerous hidden precipices, resurging childhood trauma and more—all while trying to maintain our soundness of mind. We have no supplies, no emergency rations, no lifelines. It's just me and the camera crew, our filming equipment, and one pocketknife. Foraging for meals won't be a problem, given the bodies—or rather, the rich resources that surround us now on the vast concrete.

Locating a viable water source, however, will certainly pose some difficulties.

LOT 666 has its tricks and trials, and many adventurers before us have lost themselves in its devious trappings. But if you've seen this show before, and if you know me, dear Watchers, be sure that no obstacle could hinder us, no hurdle is too great to climb, and there is absolutely nothing to worry about.

And to all newcomers: There is nothing to fear. We will survive.

Let's go.

So, we have officially entered the Trail. It appears to be a regular abandoned lot, with a mid- sized apartment building at the center, three stories, plus the half-rotted whale carcass attached to the left wall. The meat is not edible, so we won't bother looking into those parts. Don't worry about it. The whale is already dead. Dead like your dreams of a better world.

Moving on. It's a dark and terrible night, but lucky for us, the full moon offers enough light to navigate the barbed wire.

Survival Tip #1: *Watch out for venomous snakes in the shadows; they know best how to hurt you.*

We're coming up on the building entrance now. Door's unlocked; we can just walk in. This time of year, the ceiling glows, pulsing blood red. The floors are damp and sticky. That's typical.

And the hallway stretches farther than you might expect.

If you look from the outside, you'll find this building should have nine apartment units, three on every floor, despite its seemingly countless rooms. So long as you remember this, you're safe.

Tip #2: *No matter what, do not open more than three doors per floor.*

Now, look what we have here. "Absolute Drinking Water." You'll find a bunch of these laying around corners, but do not drink them under any circumstances. See the green label? It's a trick. The color and patterns are similar to most harmless PET bottles. Look closer between the ridges and you'll see the mix of impurities—the microplastics, the algal bloom, the tears shed in grief and desperation. Insanely toxic. A single drop has the potency to kill ten angels.

Speaking of angels. Here's a sign. We're inside apartment *2b*, and the kitchen is covered in angel feces—we've entered angel territory. The stench is indistinguishable from normal sewage.

You could eat this as is, if you're starving, or you could roast the feces over a fire and give it a good char, for flavor. I don't hear flapping, but just in case, I've got my knife ready.

Tip #5,289: *Angels are known to charge their prey at first sight. If one grabs you, you're dead. Always good to be alert.*

The staircase to the third floor has been blocked by a

pileup of human skeletons, so we'll have to find some other way to proceed. How have we not triggered a bone avalanche yet?

The second-floor utility closet leads to the front yard. I'm not quite sure if this is the same dimension as our own, though. Better safe than sorry.

We still haven't found potable drinking water. At this rate, we're going to be in a lot of trouble. If luck is still on our side, we'll stumble into an angel and fight it for its fluid sac.

We'll have to make a detour through the whale carcass, after all.

I was just a kid when I first went through LOT 666. After my parents' divorce, I'd run away from home and end up here, somehow. The apartment walls were green. Like a forest. The whale was alive, then, but it was dying. It had eaten too many bullets and poisoned the water. Now there are only dead things. That's why the angels are so angry, I suppose. They can't hear people praying anymore. Like I said before, those dreams are dead.

We've reached the third floor via the whalebone tunnel. The floors are flooded with clear liquid—not water. It's slightly yellowish and smells sweet. Amniotic fluid? In any case, we'll have to quench our thirst somehow. Now I remember—when I came here as a child, I met an angel who cut open its belly, just so I could have something to drink. I can't believe I'd forgotten. I wonder if I could meet that angel again, who was so unlike the rest of its kind.

And well, what do you know, we're finally at the rooftop.

The journey was rough and messy, but we made it. The emergency ladder should appear to us now—it only lets people down, never up. If you lose your footing, you'll fall straight into the depths of the earth, never to be found again.

That's it for us tonight. Thanks for tuning in to this episode of *SURVIVE*. I'm your host Meifong, I'm still alive, and I haven't lost my mind.

To anyone watching. If you're still out there.

Try to survive.

DISCOURSES ON THE SEVEN-HEADED MONKEY

TIM LIEDER

Every Wednesday evening at a certain Baker Street residence, Nigel Thorne, a man of honorable lineage and unfortunate facial hair presented himself to the splendid domicile of the brilliantly eccentric Lord Ridgely, explorer, billiards enthusiast and patron of three ballet companies, who just happened to be 45th in line for the throne. The civilians who witnessed Nigel's ritual visit would speak of duels and passionate regret. Some even mentioned the lovely doomed Lady Katherine Happerlyn by name—who would dress as a man and found herself at the receiving end of one of Nigel's youthfully drunk fists. According to the most enthusiastic of gossips, a duel had taken Lady Katherine's life and Young Nigel Thorne had been ostracized from society with the typical shunning and non-invitations.

It may prove anti-climatic to learn that the friendship between the infamous Nigel Thorne and the honorable Lord Ridgely sprang from a simple longing for days when the empire was truly blessed with inexpensive spices and imported giraffes. The gentlemen bonded in faith over a time of Great Men when chartism, radicalism, reform bills, tithe bills, and infinite discrepancy for acid jargon remained safely far away in the House of Commons, and never ventured within the view of a carriage ride to the House of Lords. They spoke daringly of a blessed decade when the colonial office was safe from blind obstructions, fatal indolences, pedantry, imbecility, jungle thinking, humanism and vile status seekers. The two men congregated in Lord Ridgely's richly furnished apartment to address times long past when life was extravagant and humanity did not worship the survival of the fittest jackanape.

Inevitably, their communication spun and twisted to the discourse of the seven-headed monkey.

Lord Ridgely encountered the seven-headed monkey in Rhodesia on his 18th birthday. Every head was uglier than poverty. The encounter greeted Lord Ridgely long before Rhodesia received the name and became utterly ravished by imperial inevitability. The land and the monkey represented an exquisitely haunting revelation.

According to Lord Ridgely, the wretched creature had inhabited the sacred spring of the Elysium Jungle. The power of speech, the authority of persuasion and the

monkey's magical paw rendered its kingly position involute. Lord Ridgely once spent eight days explicating the seven-headed monkey without sleep or food. Daily, he described a single head in detail and then on the eighth day, he took to praising the monkey as a calculative symphony of autocratic dissipation. Upon completion of the discourse, he honored the quintessential seventh head with loving poesy, before succumbing to the long-anticipated nap that offered his guests a sweet departure.

Without discovery, Nigel had invested in American companies and enjoyed witnessing his money grow a hundredfold. Whereas the peers of his class were suffering their family fortunes to disappear in the diamond mines of the Congo and the Indian troubles, Nigel was handing pound notes to a banker possessed of moral turpitude that allowed him to secure a fortuitous bounty in the stormy petrels of the former colonies. Sir Nigel Thorne, who had traced his lineage through malcontents and unfortunate lords—many of whom found their heads on spikes—was suitably ashamed of his inability to maintain his family's tragic inheritance. Nigel Thorne had been expected to wear his family shame with a dissolute smile and self-incriminating tales of forlorn poverty. Had fairness directed the world, Squire Thorne would have been an entertaining failure in the gentlemen's club alongside fading nobility who spent their days chattering about Impressionists and gilded lilies and the unfortunate working conditions of the common man. At the very least, he should have ventured an opinion about the German royal family.

Instead, Sir Nigel Thorne quietly counted his money

and waxed poetic when confounded with profane vanities and vain profanities. The tales of Lady Katherine were such barnstormers that eventually her unfortunate death was placed at the feet of Nigel to explain his anti-social reverence for the fantasies of a crystal life. In truth, the fleeting life of Lady Katherine Happerlyn, adventurer and brawler, had originated in a penny dreadful collection, the last one distributed three years after Nigel's birth. The series had been such an infamous pandemic that rumors of the unfortunate Lady Katherine, Kate to her friends, of which there were many, delighted and obsessed multitudes in the gathering society. The few who knew her literary origins forgot the books in the recollection and repetition. Nigel's attempt to dissuade the worthy gentlemen and privileged wives from her praises yielded the consequence of Nigel entering the fiction in the form of a duel where he lived in shame. All in all, Nigel Thorne did not hate his infamy as the man who killed Lady Kate, even if her last novel had made it distinctly clear that she was living in the Moors of Scotland, happily retired after a nasty fight with the king of the vampires.

Even Lord Ridgely kept the legend alive. He boldly and conspiratorially told Sir Nigel that he never cared for Lady Katherine Lockely Happerlyn. He found her habit of running around dressed as the pirate prince Sir William Baine to be in the poorest taste. He did not refer to the duel directly, but he did say that shooting such a woman should not have been a sin per se; Lady Katherine was very beautiful and well-connected, which could only render her actions infinitely more reprehensible. In the secret and sacred places between the fictions, Sir Nigel sincerely wished that Lord Ridgely would not stop thinking that Nigel had engineered her unfortunate fate.

Without Nigel's knowledge, Lord Ridgely was one of the few members of Society who knew that she was fiction and only spoke of her as a person because the books had enchanted his youth. He also felt that Sherlock Holmes really should restrict his cocaine binges to special occasions and even wrote a letter to the Times for the edification of Mr. Holmes, only to discover to his eternal consternation that the great detective had only recently perished from an unfortunate tumble.

The second head glistened with furry malice, disheveled as if recently washed in lye. It possessed dull, droopy eyes and a sad slackened jaw. The second head could simultaneously brush its teeth and snarl. All of your sleep died and your energy faded in the eyes of the second head. The strains of a dream whispered poor with time grinding out routine. Most preferred to face the head only upon the imbibing of Turkish coffee, cocaine or the blackest tea.

Lord Ridgely noted that it was impossible to look upon the second head without exasperation crawling up one's soul. It offered dreams of black glowing girls, the burning slender beauty of bodies destined for joy and flowers only to crash illusory joy in favor of the reality of steel and trains. When its green eye fell upon you, you saw your life in spoons of sugar, rubber stamps and paper, so much paper. When the black eye found you, the simplest lessons eluded every attempt. Mystics sought the black eye, unaware that it only existed in

tangent with the green eye, in perfect affection of loathsome and vicious hope.

Together, the eyes fostered special desolation. Preachers sought demonic succour. Tailors tried to shoot pigeons for their feathers. Kings would spit in public and murderers wrote invoices. Yet all the desire flopped away once the second head opened his mouth and whistled. Lord Ridgely swore that when he heard the first trains going through Bristol, the train whistle was an exact replication of that ungodly sound from the second head's mouth.

Nigel accepted his fate as an outcast. As a child, he hated the books, the games, and the pipe tobacco of his peers. Most mornings, he would leave his house, visit the club and pretend to commiserate with his fellow barons and dukes as they fretted over lost fortune. From such a perch, he would descend with a promise to patronize the lowliest Whitechapel brothels, only to slink to the bank to monitor his considerable investments. Later in the afternoon, he held congress with merchants of low character-spice importers, rope factory owners, suppliers to street vendors and Americans. Many enjoyed his company but found him both snooty and snotty. He dared not speak of the seven-headed monkey in the cortex of daily financial intercourse.

Most nights Lord Ridgely wanted to speak of the sixth head with its young eyes and deep wrinkles. It donned grandeur with a crown the color of ancient rivers. Its mouth did roar. In sweet eager anticipation, it could see infinite hydrogen. The sixth head drooled as if ready to die but smirked eager for vibrant door slamming. That head had pimples shining

in the yellow moonlight arrayed and pulsing to celebrate an apocalyptic throne.

Nigel's wife welcomed his friendship with Lord Ridgely with an attitude of firm discomfort. Oscar Wilde had only recently left the vulgar club of the breathing. School boy hobbies were one thing but grown men should relinquish childish degeneracy. She could never comprehend the desperate width of Nigel's loneliness. There were always salons, art galleries, and medical curiosities lectured upon in great detail. She marveled at the attempts to isolate and utilize sera for passive immunization. In April, her obsession swung around to extensive studies on horses protected from a myriad genus of pneumococci.

Nigel was not one to shake his fists and rage against indignities; his vicious anti-Catholic jokes pushed her into blushing laughter and shameful guffaws. She pondered the anger that stirred under his tale of a little boy who prayed very hard for spiritual treasures but ultimately chose to just kidnap the Virgin Mary for a materialist ransom.

She did not tell that joke nor any of Nigel's humorous tales at the Irish Tolerance League. She did recite it to a suffragette friend named Matilda, who was arrested three times within the past year for throwing bricks at windows and was learning to run more quickly because of it. Dear Matilda laughed with joy but then spoke just a few minutes too long concerning the dangers of popery. Nigel's wife was sympathetic to anti-papist sentiments but not so much that she desired to pay heed to tedious history lessons.

Purple steam billowed from the monkey's fur for

daylight but upon the sun rays turning brilliant for the setting, all the purple would vanish as if never except from a single 30 degree angle, where one could see smoke flowing into angelic faults. When Lord Ridgely described the smoke-white then black then purple only to retrieve its white hue-Nigel heard footsteps, sonorous and sublime under the floorboards as if the downside up world existed in Lord Ridgely's cellar.

In their monkey discussions, the two gentlemen drank cognac. Discourse on a beatific Rhodesian monkey required sipping. When the Ridgely family commissioned a never-dying portrait, Lord Ridgely insisted upon posing in a green velvet robe whilst holding a cognac snifter. No one protested. Truthfully, most expressed relief that he was not posing over a dead lion.

The first head sparkled apple green; its eyes the color of tovu and vohu. With its mouth rigid, it spoke. The words fell upon your skin, and you simpered in the fresh blessing of eternal terraces and opera planets. The first head moved in dialogue with heavenly Mexicans and wicked Quakers. Enough water gushed from its eyes to revive Ponce de Leon. The monkey's first head shimmered radiant hazel-grove rust formless and possibly esteemed. The first eyes could only see white fire on black fire.

Lord Ridgely impressed upon visitors that he had been a youthful explorer visiting his father's diamond mines on Tuesday and an old lord on Wednesday. The chattering Lord Ridgely saw himself perpetually returning from pure faith eager to spread the monkey gospel.

Yet fanaticism did not suit Lord Ridgely. He never raised

his voice. Rarely did he break a table leg or shoot a native in anger. Never did he whip his wife. She birthed five children and quietly perished without complaint. He debated Tory politics in gentlemen's clubs and played chess with Russian emigrants, many with Jewish ancestry. In his middle years, he cultivated roses and parliament favors as he consumed his daily roasted lamb with butter scones. In the year of the Ripper, he converted to a strict vegetarian diet at the behest of a favorite radical cousin. He maintained his disconcerting faith for three years until a visit to Vienna introduced him to a feast of blood sausage and prosaic Communist verse. He met Nigel in his gentleman's club. Lord Ridgely felt an instant rapport when Sir Nigel refrained from the traditional cough and excuse of avoidance regarding Lord Ridgely's discussion of the monkey that had defined his youth and haunted his middle years.

The fourth head sprouted from darkness, small roads and ancient forests. Vengeance and envy colonized its very sharp teeth. The eyes were redder than Mohammedan devils; the tongue slithered in a glitter of muskets. The fourth head's fur smelled like Swiss chocolate and old dogs. The head brought forth every insult, injurious or indignant. The fourth head drove war and parliamentary radicalism. Withered men took up arms for duels as if youth with all its thriving hatred still gripped their souls and hands and genitals. Slights forgotten and forgiven arose with a furious leviathan.

Lord Ridgely had only looked at the head for 15 seconds. Had he allowed his gaze to linger for a second more, he would have dueled and whored his way into an unmarked grave. He

stomped a servant into a coma when the subject of the fourth head arose without diligent warning. Signs of dangerous nostalgia in Lord Ridgely rose as the servant spoke–dilating eyes, a twitch in the left cheek, a small but discernible twisting of the ring on his left middle finger–and yet, the servant refused to acknowledge his peril at his lord's consternation until the silver cane was falling upon the poor man's shoulders and skull.

Nigel allowed his wife to handle the serving staff-miscreants and rogues; often they would burn the soup or add too much curry. Tomato Florentine whisked assiduous in its overtly garlic and onion bitterness. Had Nigel laid hands upon such cretins, they would have left his employ just as easily as they left brothels when their money ran out. They were constantly seeking masters who were less prone to Nigel's gloom.

In an attempt to placate the seething mass of humanity that depended on benefice, Nigel told jokes about Pollacks and Jews and Greeks. He tried to join them in their quarters as they sang dirty Irish songs to no avail. They always shut their faces into strict obeisance upon his approach. When, purely from curiosity, he inquired about their methods of removing blood, they would answer in proper but inaccurate sentences full of cheap justice and social anomalies.

Nigel did pay special mind to one serving girl in particular, a Mary Elizabeth Downing, with blond hair and sea blue eyes-pretty as diamonds-who flirted and sashayed, skirts traveling provocative and evocative to display her leg and leaning into the scrubbing as if to offer her lovely white

breasts for Nigel's edification. Then one day when she was removing the waxy residue from a window display, Nigel refused the burden of miserable celibate inability imposed upon him by social obligation. His arms pinned her as he uttered amorous oaths. She resisted his carnal demands, but he was certain that she cried from joy. The next day she left his employ with 500 guineas, a letter of recommendation and a promise to remain silent. Never again did Nigel gaze upon her tearful visage. He wrote beatific vows on parchment that disappeared under his floorboards. One night he soaked his pillow with tears, but Mary Elizabeth could never return to ease his heavy heart.

Countless pilgrims journeyed to the remote jungle from tales and myths and rumors of the third head. The left eye sprouted vulgar tears and the right eye remained brown and dry. Teeming, shrieking life colonized its forehead in a cavalcade of tiny creatures, sparking with the utmost green exertion. The parade of roaches, bugs, insects and trilobites crawled perpetually in broad malingering splendour.

On a night in April or maybe May, Nigel arrived at Lord Rigely's house at a late hour as he had been wandering the city in a vain attempt to procure spirits from Sunday vendors. The malicious band of cutthroats and blackguards invoked legalities to persecute Nigel's adulated skull. A woman that Nigel could not recognize had accosted him with a tale of woe. She had married Lord Pagini of Florence at one point and he had thrown her to a cornucopia of dances, drinking vermouth, dice playing and chambermaid brawls before divorcing her. He insulted her with a dismissive shove. She cried copious

tears whilst holding Nigel's hand. He could only sputter out comfortable meaningless noises. He finally left the encounter feeling so small that he wondered why suicide was not the rational masculine choice. Thus he arrived at Lord Ridgely's sitting room at an hour that could not suit either man.

Lord Rigely did not mind the lack of spirits and pushed forth a vintage absinthe drink flavored with cherry that he had procured in Paris. Nigel's despondent retelling of the woman's tale was not sated. Perhaps, he had killed the Lady Happerlyn, and while he was confessing, he most certainly pushed the dear Inspector Holmes from that waterfall. He never cared for the man.

Lord Ridgely listened to his confession with the serenity of angelic industry. He waited for the burning phrases to depart from Nigel's lips. His smile remained fixed as Nigel paused in his recitation. Lord Ridgely took the opportunity to speak about the seventh head.

The monkey's seventh head mixed dismay with ennui and terror to form a magnificent amalgamation of disfigurements. Mismatched eyes, visible smoke, hands growing from foreheads, where pimples, discolored fur and black spit mingled; even if one knew that the head should have been terrible, full of metaphysical theological significance. The head rendered all disgust academic in the brilliant ecstatic leisure. The seventh head was the monkey in its most restive, as if the pain, striving, disappointment and frustration could be unholy sainted in a sterilizing breeze.

Lord Ridgely strove constantly for the seventh head. He could never truly render the details since the broad strokes

made his audience sick from imagination. Yet the feeling broke from petty phrases and clumsy metaphors to blanket the listener in a bounty of happy future nostalgia. Merely observe the way the fungal passion blew from its nose. HeLord Ridgely allowed no discussion, no debate when words sought vainly to describe the final head. On the nights when Lord Ridgely weakened with drink and factory fog climbed to his bed and rubbed his bleeding rashes, a few words to describe broken hearts and the blessedly grotesque seventh head eased his reedy cough.

After discoursing upon the seventh head, the wind spoke to Lord Ridgely mournfully with nostalgic tunes of Irish children dying from cholera. That night, he abruptly ended his recitation and moved to the steps. As Lord Ridgely did not take his leave, Nigel assumed that he would return. Nigel sat in the chill of the house searching the library and blue flower wallpaper for memories of dead lovers and Turkish baths. Mostly, he sat in his chair pondering the seven-headed monkey and its fate should it be captured and placed in a zoo. He thought of children crying and ladies throwing off their petticoats. Nigel was old enough to remember that every potential world-betraying event that should shock and open the mind to new possibilities never lived up to promise. The mysteries of the East became a series of parlour games while the merciless and precise poetry of Omar Khayyam provided background noise to schoolboy peccadillo.

Sir Nigel smoked a pipe and brooded over municipal injustices, while Lord Ridgely experienced his favorite and final heart attack. The nobleman was leaving his body or

shutting himself into black permanent dreamless sleep. A maid shrieked when she saw his eyes open and felt his skin cold. She was young and unaccustomed to cadavers. She liked Lord Ridgely because he was always kind and even prudish.

Nigel attended the memorial service and gazed upon the mourners for the brother of Lady Happerlyn as if such a person could exist in the Gilded Age. He admired the paintings in the sitting room. They were not Pre-Raphaelite and yet embraced the style. The family posed Lord Ridgely's body sitting up to obtain the final photograph for posterity.

Sir Nigel's children attended boarding schools where they received the finest education and best buggery available in England's green earth. His wife held meetings for the sisterhood and gossip never escaped his attention. On moon-deprived nights, he would wander the streets as if there was another Lord Ridgely to impart the wisdom of the seven-headed monkey. At moments of clarity, he would walk into pubs and approach the drunk on the far stool, the one with the collapsing corpuscles. With a serious look and a catch in his throat, Nigel would introduce his person by stating: "I understand the fifth head."

CURSE THE DARKNESS

DIE BOOTH

It's worse in the winter.

The dark freezes him as much as the cold, Matt's ability to do anything fading with the daylight, like a pet bird claimed by sleep whenever its cage is covered.

It's not that he's scared of the dark, even, like Rosie tentatively suggests. He just hates it, with every fibre of his being.

"It's funny, really. I mean – look at you." Rosie says, gesturing to Matt's all-black everything, the skull-shaped ring on his middle finger. Matt pointedly displays the ring in reply, but Rosie just smiles, mildly, like she does. And Matt knows that Rosie means funny-strange, not funny-hilarious, but nothing about this feels funny at all when you're the one living through it.

S.A.D. to go with his sad. Somehow, living with Rosie makes it even harder to deal with, which is funny-strange, seeing as Rosie is sunshine personified, a living light-ray directing her loving golden beam always into Matt's darkness. But the darkness just swallows it up, insatiable and starving, nothing to reflect back: being with Rosie doesn't make Matt feel brighter – it just highlights how unalike they are, reminds him every day that he's different, makes him wonder just what the hell is wrong with him.

"There's nothing wrong with you," Rosie says, gently. It's August, still summer, and the day is sunny. Saturday, afternoon, they're both off work, and Matt should be feeling fantastic. But the brighter the light, the darker the shadow it casts. Already, in the afternoon, the shadows are lengthening, anxiety pricking as he watches autumn lurking just over the horizon. The thought tracks into his brain and stays, a train chugging round and round and round, filling his head with filthy smoke: every step towards daylight is ultimately just a step closer to night again.

"I know there's nothing wrong with me," Matt says, because he *knows*, he just doesn't *feel*. There *must* be a way to break this cycle. He tips his head back, face towards the sun like a daisy, feeling the heat and the red blaze of brightness even through his closed lids. If only it were like this, always.

Rosie takes his hand, where it's resting next to her on the bench, circling his palm with a gentle thumb. "Maybe you could see someone? A therapist. A hypnotist, maybe?"

"Maybe." Matt says. He's seen doctors before, NHS

and private. Psychiatrists and counsellors and so-called gender specialists, talking therapy and CBT. He doesn't need medicine. What he needs is a miracle.

"Yeah. A hypnotist." Matt says, and he almost believes himself. A witch is kind of like a hypnotist, right? It's all just made-up nonsense to take advantage of the gullible and the desperate, and Matt figures he's half of that at least.

"I'm proud of you." Rosie says, and beams her brilliant smile, and Matt only feels a little bit bad for lying, because isn't he taking a step towards helping himself, after all?

Who knew that witches have offices like shrinks? It's not what Matt signed up for, but he's here now, early even, and that's an achievement in itself. At this stage, it's easier to stay than go, and the chair he's lounged on with its inoffensive, oatmeal-coloured upholstery is surprisingly comfortable for a poky little waiting room in a Georgian townhouse shared with a solicitor's and a boutique travel consultant. The witch is on the top floor. The sign on the door doesn't say anything except her name: Kerry Hughes.

Matt is bored. He zones out and stares, through the slats of the blinds that only hint at a weak white sky and the brick wall of the building opposite. Checks his phone, scrolling until he finds something upsetting enough to jolt him out of it. Peels off his phone case, polishing the back of his naked mobile with a corner of his shirt, suddenly an imperative and consuming task. Over too soon.

The thoughts crowd back in, elbowing past the ongoing

babble in his head, *I am cleaning my phone I am waiting for the witch what the hell's a witch supposed to be anyway remember when you killed that frog when you were little no don't just stamped on it that window blind is so dusty it's like my phone case I wonder if she'll have a hat remember how it felt maybe you should kill a cat stop it's half-past already she's late what if she hates me what if she can tell how long does it-*

Matt squeezes his eyes shut, then opens them at the hollow thud of his heart as he's plunged into darkness. Balling a fist, he thumps the top of this thigh, his leg jittering up and down. *Shut up shut up shut up shut-*

The door opens.

"So, you understand what I've told you?" says the guy. Witch. Kerry.

Matt nods. "I thought that witches were women." If he thinks about it now, he'd have to admit to himself that he's been thinking about it like, a lot, ever since he entered the office, to the point that he has, in fact, possibly *not* understood everything that Kerry has just told him because he's been too fixated on the Kerry being a dude thing. Which makes him feel really terrible to be honest, that he's assumed someone's gender, given that he's trans himself, not that Kerry knows that, at least he hopes that Kerry can't somehow sense it with witch powers or something...

Matt takes a slow breath, and says quickly, "Not that men can't like, do the stuff and that, I just thought 'witch' was for women and 'wizard' was for men, like waiter and waitress. Or is it 'warlock' for men? Anyway. And, like. Your name."

Kerry smiles. He's got combed-back black hair and very blue eyes. *You should kiss him*, the ever-present voice in Matt's head suggests. Matt grits his teeth. "It's Irish," Kerry says, then repeats, "You understand what I've told you?"

"Yeah." Kerry is looking at him, expectantly. Matt cannot let him down. "You can't do the, thing. The spell." It makes him feel sort of stupid even saying the word, but in for a penny and all that, and this has cost a lot more than a penny so he best make the most of it. "I have to do it myself. You'll email me the map and the words and stuff."

"And remember, the most important thing. Be respectful at all times and when you come up with the wording of your intention, you must be very, *very* specific as to what you want to happen."

Kerry has square-framed glasses and a suit jacket on over a grey jumper. He looks exactly like a therapist. He's wearing a ring on his left ring finger, but it doesn't look like a wedding ring… Matt looks up, and nods. "Yep. Specific. Got it."

"Good luck, Matt. Let me know how it goes." Kerry stands to see him out. "I hope that you find what you're looking for."

It's not that he's underprepared, it's just that Matt is used to winging it. He has prepared, in that he read the email that Kerry sent, and he brought out offerings to the right place (woods, ten-minute car journey away) at the right time (night, full moon on a Monday to be precise) and he's being 'respectful of the process' in that he's like, doing it, isn't he? Lowering his backpack over the gate, he climbs over after it, a jagged creep of unease spidering up his spine at the night

and the quiet and the woods crouched beside him. It's darker among the trees. Twigs crack beneath his step, and things rustle in the bushes. Foxes, maybe, or rabbits. The birds must all be roosting though, as he's not heard a single one since he set foot inside the woods.

This should be far enough. After all, Kerry didn't specify how far in he had to go and one silent, tree-lined clearing is the same as the next. Sweat prickles the back of his neck as he opens his bag and lines up his offerings on a fallen log, bark flaking half-rotten as it submerges into the undergrowth.

A bowl, a carton of milk, a squeezy bottle of honey, some bread. He didn't have time to go to the shops and buy new like the instructions said, but the bowl's a nice one and the bread was fresh yesterday and nobody drinks full-fat milk any more anyway.

Pouring the milk out, it makes him think about hedgehogs when he was little. That was what you fed them, back in the old days, bread and milk. Now it's dog food or meal worms because bread and milk is actually really bad for them or something and…

Matt's knees crack as he stands up. His head spins, sending the leeched-grey streaks of trees around him expanding and contracting like a 1920s cartoon, like he's inside a zoetrope. Must have stood up too quickly. He takes a deep breath, willing away the unease as the dark seems to crawl closer: this is why he's doing all this.

"So. Hiya." His voice sounds oddly hollow in the quiet night. He only feels a bit stupid, talking to himself, here in the waiting gloom. "I brought you this. I hope you're not

hedgehogs. So if you, you know, exist, actually. Then." He nudges the bowl of bread and honey-milk further along the log. What does he want? Might as well just go for it. "I want it to be light. I guess, just for me. But, no more darkness. I want it to be day all the time, so I can stop feeling tired and get stuff done."

Quiet. Nothing. Not even a breath of wind through the trees.

Matt says, as a quite sincere after-thought, "Please?" But the whole thing feels suddenly even dumber than it did on the way here. He'd thought perhaps it would feel… *something*. Symbolic? Psychological? Like when you write down your problems and burn them and it actually helps a tiny bit for a while. Now he just has to drive home and leave a bowl in the woods, which feels a bit like littering if he's honest, and he liked that bowl, but probably animals will eat the bread and he can come back for the bowl another day.

"Ow!" Ducking sharply, he squeezes his eyes shut. Presses a knuckle against the sharp prick of pain behind his left lid. Damn midges, something in his eye. He squints it open, watering, and sees the trees around him waltz, swimming in and out of his vision like a mirage, silhouetted against a sapphire sky.

Something isn't right.

Matt staggers, throwing out a hand. He catches a trunk, the bark rough and grating beneath his palm. The air smells of moss and soil and something achingly sweet turning to rot, like milk and honey left to spoil. Tears stream down his cheeks as Matt slits open his eyes to a blazing day. Blinking, he checks his phone: 9.15pm.

In the sunny green canopy overhead, a bird starts to sing, and then another, and another, until they are almost deafening.

Matt knows instantly that he's made a mistake.

It's too weird, too alien, as he stumbles back through the woods, eyes still streaming, and sits in the car trying to calm his panicky breaths. The pain is quick to pass, at least, but the reality remains: it's broad daylight at nearly 10pm. How can this have worked? The only realistic conclusion is that it's all in his mind, but then how -?

In a trance, Matt puts the car in gear and eases off the handbrake. Reverses out of the little parking area without putting on the lights, his vision clear as morning. A passing car blares a warning horn at him as he indicates to pull out onto the road, and he flicks the headlights on, the clamour of his thoughts for once stunned into silence.

Silenced by the light.

Maybe, however this has happened, it's not so bad after all.

It's OK until he tries to sleep.

When he gets in, it's nearly 11, because he spent so long sat in shock in the car, staring mutely at the minutes ticking past on the clock. And the world remained the same constant brightness, despite the moon overhead and the stars just visible in the sky, as if the street had suddenly been flooded with electric illumination from some unseen source.

Rosie is already in bed. Matt is quiet, by sheer force of

habit. He stands in the middle of the kitchen floor and pushes his thumb and forefinger against his closed eyelids as hard as he dares, watching the kaleidoscope of hot green and neon pink and blazing white strobe in waterlilies of pressure against a background of not black, but sodium yellow. Removing his fingers, but keeping his eyes closed, it's the same. Bright, buttery light, like staring at a lamp with his eyes open. "This isn't what I meant." His voice comes out as a whisper, because even if he's having a crisis, Rosie is still sleeping. Maybe Matt *is* dreaming. Maybe he's having a breakdown. Maybe he can just sleep it off. It'll all be better in the morning.

Climbing carefully beneath the well-lit duvet, Matt goes to turn the bedside light off, then remembers. He watches Rosie for a while, sleeping. The soft rise and fall of her chest. The flutter of blonde lashes against her cheeks, and her gently parted lips, all in perfect clarity, untouched by shadow. He closes his eyes, and lets the light wash over him.

By the fourth day, Matt knows that this isn't something he can adapt to. He thinks that he's slept, in a vague, passing-out-from-exhaustion type of way, but it turns out that trying to get proper rest when you're cursed with the equivalent of a torch shone into your clamped-open eyes twenty-four-seven is incredibly difficult.

Cursed. He's beginning to believe it.

He knows somehow with fluttering guts and a childhood full of books he'd been too young to read, that Kerry wouldn't answer his phone-calls or emails. When he visits the office in the Georgian townhouse to find the top-floor door locked

and only the ghost of the name-plate lingering in scrubbed-off adhesive on the glass, he isn't even surprised.

Rosie notices, of course. She listens patiently, with a sweet little line of concern carved between her brows that makes Matt feel miserably guilty. It's concern for the state of his sanity, of course, not for a magical spell gone wrong, and the knowledge that he can't even make the one he loves most in the world understand what's going on fills him with the bleakest, most vivid loneliness he's ever felt. It's all there, under a spotlight that won't switch off. Everything that is wrong with his life.

"Maybe," Rosie says, gently, "the darkness is there for a reason. Like sadness, to happiness. Things only have true value in contrast."

"Stuff's gotta suck so we know what's cool?" Matt says, wretchedly, and Rosie kisses the top of his head. Matt's eyes water. He holds them wide open and tries not to blink, letting the hateful light flood in. It makes no difference either way: may as well keep them open and look his mistakes dead-on. "But there's no darkness, not any more. It's all bright. It's like the light *is* darkness now." Rosie nods, and bites her lip. It looks like her eyes are watering, too.

Even in his dreams, Matt can't escape the light. He's starting to lose track of what's waking and what's dreaming, as if he's sleeping with his eyes open.

He goes back to the woods and pleads, but the birdsong sounds like jeering and the bowl he'd left there is gone. Life passes in a dazzling daze. Rosie is worried, but she can't understand why Matt won't go to the doctor again, won't try

just one more referral, just one more counsellor.

He tries to turn off the light.

The voice in his head whispers it, over and over again, more insistently than it's done in years, but Matt wracks his brain for another way.

Summer slides into autumn, leaves falling and crushing underfoot in mellow buttery drifts, black-spotted with damp. The air grows sharper at the edges, a scent of cold to it. The light lies. Even in torrential October rain the steely sky is perversely luminous, casting short, defined shadows from no natural source. And Matt tries to enjoy it – it's what he wanted – but his mind is falling apart like wet mud.

Sleep masks don't help. Closing his eyes at all is pointless. Sleeping pills knock him out and leave him groggy in the morning, hungover from dreams of glaring flames. He can't even shade his eyes against it: the light is uniform and unchanging and every shadow he steps into flees, as though the source of the light has changed angles to chase him.

He wants the darkness back.

The first time he really thinks about a final solution is when he's submerged in the bath. The tiny bubbles that silver up from his nose, the pressed corners of his lips, gleam like mercury in the bright, underwater silence. It's beautiful, really. It roars in his ears like white noise, calming. Eyes closed or open, the brightness persists, turning the undulating surface to busy ripples of light. His lungs are starting to burn: he's been under too long. Black spots start to cluster the corners of his vision and even as his body screams for air, his mind clings to the darkness forming, craving it almost more than

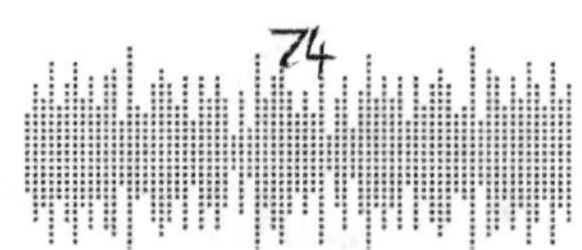

his animal vessel demands survival.

Almost.

He surfaces with a great dragging gasp, pushing his dripping hair back from his forehead. Dries himself with - for a few minutes - a quiet mind.

Later, an email alert pings up on his screen, with the name 'Kerry Hughes' and Matt almost drops his phone in his haste to open it, his palms slick and heart battering. It's a reply to his last email and contains only two words: no refunds.

I don't want a refund, I just want answers. Please. How do I stop it? His hands shake as he presses 'send.'

A few moments later, the response arrives. 550 5.1.1 Address not found.

Matt lets the phone drop to the floor with a soft thud. It lies there, on the russet-coloured pile, every carpet fibre delineated clear and crisp in the forever midday light. His mind buzzes like flies.

"Are you alright, love?" Rosie asks.

Matt's mouth shapes the words, "Yeah. I'm fine." His tongue spits them out.

Even Rosie, the brightest point of his floodlit light, can't keep him here suffering this torture day after day-day-day and never any night. He pens his regrets and sorries and *I love you but*, in a trance, folds the paper and signs it. Rosie's name, sloping, is barely legible with how weak he feels now, everything gone faded in the light.

Drowning is no way to go, but he can't afford to take chances. He's seen that blissful darkness once, tantalising glimpses of it in the corners of his fading vision in the bathtub.

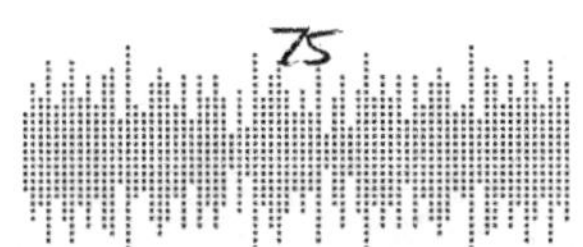

Matt keeps it in mind, clings to it like a lifebuoy as he walks to the apex of the bridge. None of this feels real. The sunny midnight trees sway and moan, weeping leaves into the rushing river. The water smells cold, even from way up here, mingled with the spice of rotting leaves, the damp scent of stone. It's easy to climb up on the balustrade. The rail is low – too low, really. Kids jump off it in the summer and swim. Nobody jumps off in the middle of the night in autumn when the river is high. Nobody is around. Sitting with legs dangling, Matt takes a last look up and down the bright river bank, then lets himself go.

Impact punches the breath from him; the shock of bone-deep cold making him inhale, cough, choke. It's instant. The current tugs him, gleeful, strong, beneath the bridge and away. It happens so fast. Falling, then submerging, less frightening than he'd feared. The tumble of water glitters above as he sinks but feels like he's floating, chrome ribbons of light fluttering in a diminishing sky, all of his senses dulled, *all* of them, as he sees it – the darkness, creeping in.

He thinks of Rosie.

Everything goes black.

It's been a while.

Matt feels like maybe he's asleep, or dreaming, or perhaps just waking. He feels rested for the first time in a long time, as he opens his eyes, or dreams that he opens his eyes. How long has he been under? Where is he? Everything is dark, and he feels strange – weightless, in silence, unable to discern any smell. But he feels calm. Comfortable. It's dark, still, but it's getting lighter, like dawn behind closed curtains. He's in bed, he thinks, drifting, just about to wake up next to Rosie, all of this just a dreadful dream.

The darkness recedes. Takes grey shape. A tunnel. Where on earth is he, in a tunnel? Matt thinks of the woods, and the witch, and the spell. If magic is real, then what else is? He can make the walls out more clearly now, the stone coming into definition as the darkness fades.

A light at the end of the tunnel, getting brighter and brighter. And brighter.

THE SUN APPROACHES EVERY SUMMER

AKIS LINARDOS

I first noticed it three summers ago, but none of the villagers believed me.

I awoke in my house, feeling warmer than usual, the dust of my bed sticking to my back through layers of sweat. The air was drier, thick with bitter dust. Once outside, I squinted at the sun, wrapped my thumb and index finger around its flickering outline to pretend I'm snatching it like a marble from the sky. I did this every morning, but this time the distance between my fingers was slightly larger.

Why was I doing this every morning? It was my daily gift to my wife. My mom taught me that if I was lucky enough to find myself a good woman, I should treat her better than my father treated her (he abandoned Mom, flew off to the sky before we'd even met). Mom told me to shower my wife in jewels bright as the sun. And although I didn't love my wife as a man is supposed to, I knew she was a good woman and a great friend. And since I had no money for jewels, I gave her the sun every morning.

But this morning the size was wrong.

Now, how could I be so sensitive to the slightest difference that would boggle an alchemist to distinguish under a magnifying lens? Simple. I was born this way.

My first memory was an ant crawling along my baby arms. I probably was two years old when I held it in my fingers. It tipped its antennas up at me, and I squinted, focusing on the tiny thing and measuring its antennae against the scar along my thumb—the one the village doctor gave me when he cut me. I never understood how cutting me helped, but he was confident it did, and more importantly he was an adult and knew better.

This scar never healed and never shrunk, and I could use it to measure things, so as a child I grew fascinated with comparing sizes. Other kids found it strange, and it's why I never had friends. While they picked teams to play catch, I was the annoying one pointing out the chance for success based on how long their legs and arms were, and how that related to the ball size.

They never got it, and treated me cruelly.

Years later, one of them became my wife's boyfriend. She didn't know I knew, but I was happy for her. I really was.

She'd been a great friend if nothing else, and had every right to pursue activities I didn't care to pursue with her.

And I was truly sad to see her boyfriend die of heatstroke first when the sun creeped closer next summer.

Two summers ago, the sun had grown even bigger—I could only 'snatch' it if I stretched my index and thumb to maximum distance between one another—but it was also redder.

The villagers noticed the size difference by then, and they felt the heat, too, so they stayed home and kept their windows open for the breeze to soothe them. They couldn't see the changed color though. I saw it. It was subtle, but my vision was too precise to miss it.

As a child I trained my eye by gathering flowers of all kinds and arranging them by size and shade. Although it wasn't entirely correct to say I gathered them. The flowers followed me.

I sort of willed them to, pretending to be a wizard. I'd extend my arm over the window, and beckon them, hoping they would levitate toward me. My mother mentioned my father would do such things to impress her so I thought if he could, why not me? I did not expect it to work. It was an idle game of imagined hope. But soon the petals flew off their daisies and roses and floated over the window, nesting on my palms.

It brought a smile to my face, and I kept doing it, until the neighbor's garden was winter-bare in the middle of spring, and she came screaming at our door. My mother told

her off though, because I hadn't left the house in days as I was sick with fever and she had no right to make outrageous accusations anyway. There was no such thing as magic.

I felt guilty for hiding my crime, but at my age, you got excited when discovering such things. And I was afraid of the mayor. He had done terrible things to witches before, even if the priest insisted witches were not real. These two always disagreed, and Mother said it was because the priest was too honest that the mayor won every time. A master of lies, and it's how he got voted for as long as I had been alive.

Still, I was unable to resist experimenting with flowers. The more I played with them the more sensitive I grew to color; even addicted to it. I'd arrange the petals on the street, leaving messages hoping my father soaring through the skies would appreciate the meticulous detail to the alignment of shades and hue. All the messages said the same thing, *we need you*, or, *Mother needs you*. Which was true. And maybe my father could defend my mother from the villagers that began accusing her of witchcraft.

I'd also color my scar by rubbing petals and leaves against it. It sucked all the color and stayed yellow and green for days.

I still had the scar as an adult, and it often took the color of the spices I used in cooking, so now it was red since I started using paprika in my dishes. It dug into the scar's creases and crusted it until it changed color. I'd nibble my thumb now and then, tasting it. When others offered me food, like in the village tavern, and the meat lacked spices as it always did, I dug my thumb deep into its cooked flesh and wiggled it there, trying to spread the spice.

Wash it, my wife demanded one day.

Now, I loved her as a friend, and I knew she was agitated and in mourning for the dead boyfriend even though she wouldn't admit it to me, so I respectfully declined.

That night, I hugged her in bed, hoping that would calm her, so she wouldn't cry in her sleep. And since I hadn't done so in a long time, it seemed strange how her elbows shoved against my ribs, and how her skin stuck to my fingertips.

One summer ago, I awoke mid-afternoon—or maybe night, it made no difference anymore—body warm and so sweaty I could feel my palm creases. I stepped over my wife's shrunken corpse and went outside to see the sun so large I had to use both hands to fit its outline.

There was no longer a point in me giving it to her. Even if she weren't dead, I doubt she would appreciate it, seeing it was the sun that killed her.

I wasn't sure why the heat never hurt me as it had my fellow villagers, most of whom were suffering severe heatstroke. Could be the droplets that clung to me, keeping the surface of my skin wet before they evaporated. These droplets came from the clouds. I was famished, after the drought had already weakened the crops and sucked up the river, so I reached up to the clouds every day, like a kid playing wizard again. Rain, rain, rain, come back to the village, I wished. Father, make rain return. But no rain came. Instead, a rivulet floated down from the clouds, and when it touched my fingers it slowly enveloped me. Membrane-like.

It was the most refreshing feeling of my life.

The sun loomed larger and red as an apple, evaporating the droplets from the back of my neck as I thumped along the flagstone-paved streets. No bird chirped, no cat mewled, not a single merchant praised his wares. There were only my footsteps and the whooshing of dry wind.

In that quiet contemplation I wondered: Was I a monster for not feeling anything about my wife being dead? Was I a monster for feeling a sense of relief for not being asked to perform activities beyond my interests, nor co-inhabit a space in ways that never aligned with me?

I sure felt like a monster, but there was no one to judge me as one anymore. No one to confess my disgusting thoughts to.

We reach the summer of now, with the village folk shrunk like raisins on the streets, arranged one next to the other with arms laying on the sides.

I did not bury anyone. I hoped to bury my wife once the priest healed, but he never did. He died soon after the mayor, who had died soon after the village doctor, who had died soon after her forty-four patients.

Now I am alone.

It makes me feel special in a way. A one-man village. A little playground with no one to tell me there's no such thing as magic. No one to judge me as a demon child, no one to accuse my mother of witchcraft, and no one to burn her alive.

One by one I drag the dead villagers and align them on the street. The putrid smell is suffocating, but I've gotten used to it. Even though the sun is as large as a flying titan or

god, its heat doesn't hurt. The clouds are always beside me, come down from the sky to spread along the village like mist. As I willed them to.

I drag my wife along the street and place her beside the mayor. She is a little taller than him, and a little shorter than the doctor. It fits my vision. I still enjoy arranging things by size. What bugs me is their shade and hue constantly change, because their skin chars in the sun and blackens—in different ways for each villager.

It sort of reminds me of when they burned my mother at the stake, the way her skin wrinkled. Although unlike her, these ones don't scream. They are silent and cooperative about the arrangement.

Understandably, this would be unsettling to a standard person, but it's just not to me. I was never unsettled. I don't know why that is. Mother always said Father was never unsettled by anything either.

He came from some distant land he never described to her. She kind of wished for the perfect man upon a falling star one day, and he slowly drifted from the night sky down to her window. Skin cold, iris black as midnight—black as mine—and hands with which to shape and cook delicacies she never dreamed of. Must have gotten that from him as well.

Anyway, he returned to the sky eventually, or so my mother said. Maybe it's why I wished to pull the sky down so much. To finally meet him. Maybe.

I'll have to keep shifting the bodies around as their color changes, from bone white, to charred black and the various shades of ashen gray in between. If my father is anything like

me, he'll be a perfectionist. I wonder if he'll notice my refined message, come down and tell me what a good job I did and we can return to our true home together.

I wonder if he noticed me pulling the sun down.

Sure it was an accident, and I only figured it was me about a week ago. It's quite silly, how playing this game for my wife had such unintended consequences. Almost funny. I should've imagined this would happen, pretending to pull the sun every morning. But really? The whole sun?

It's too much to think of.

BUT THE WI-FI IS GREAT

JOHN WISWELL

It was not the first time Char was accused of this.

Oh, Jean Paul acted like he wasn't implying anything. For months, he claimed to understand asexuality, and understand that sexuality and romance weren't necessarily linked, and that he wasn't really interested in physical relationships either. Those words lasted until they moved in together. Then the idle touches started. When they spooned during movie time, his hands rested in new places. When she set boundaries, there came the negging and the puerile questions.

"What am I doing wrong?"

"What's wrong with me?"

"Aren't you even a little curious how it would feel?"

He was not the first. This was Char's third relationship

where her partner turned her asexuality from her orientation into her diagnosis. If she stayed in the apartment another week, she would break his tablet over his head.

Thank God for Raleigh. Raleigh managed a private motel in Little Tunguska, and had begged her to visit for months. When she texted that she needed a place to clear her head, his response was a gif of cartoon pearly gates flying open.

Little Tunguska was a speck of a town. It was a sun-bleached gas station, a church that was gradually sinking into the earth, and a mostly vacant strip mall that hosted only something called "Anya's Foot Readings." The most interesting sight was a pond at the bottom of a deep depression, jagged and dramatic. The land was creased and folded for yards around it, like wrinkles in the corner of a wincing eye. Char wondered what had happened to make such an impression on the earth. Tiny toads chirped along the pond's otherwise barren banks.

One left turn after the crater pond, she reached the Little Tunguska Motel. Lemonade yellow paint flecked from wooden walls, and old rainwater puddled in the retractable canvas awnings. The parking lot was a bunch of bald patches where tires carved through its gravel. She'd have to trust Raleigh that there weren't any bed bugs. If her dad was still alive, he would've freaked that she'd stay here.

Raleigh greeted her in the parking lot, where his dinged-up Elantra was the only other car. He wore a garden hose green bolo tie over a white button down shirt with long sleeves – all in the heat of May. He made Char feel underdressed in her Pride tee.

She said, "Thank you so much for having me. Are you sure you don't want me to pay?"

"Please." He swatted playfully at her forearm. "This time of year the only customers I get are the occasional pair of teens looking to spend the night out of earshot of their parents. You're going to save my sanity."

"Sanity's nice if you can get it," she said, eying the grime and crooked blinds on the windows. The place had fifteen rooms, all in a straight row. The numbers skipped from Room 12 to Room 14. That was *so* Raleigh's sense of humor.

Looking at the yellow doors gave her head a faint and fuzzy feeling. It was the sensation of her mouth in the morning if she didn't brush her teeth the night before, except the sensation climbed into her eyes.

She tried blinking it away. She was probably dehydrated from the drive.

Raleigh said, "You wouldn't guess it, but we've got ridiculous wifi. Whatever you've got? 4K? 8K? We can stream several thousand of the alphabet of your choice. And it's free."

"Really?"

"It's a town initiative. They want to get more people out here."

"Good, because I've got work I need to catch up on. Got to redesign a website by tomorrow."

"Then let's get you checked in."

Char smirked. "Can I get lucky Room 14?"

Raleigh cackled and fetched her the key.

As she dragged her bag over the threshold of the room, she felt the first slender pain in her temples, like a knife asking

to get intimate with her thoughts. That was the start of it.

She visited the soda machine for some caffeine to kill this headache.

"Nip it in the bud, Charlotte," Dad had said. When Char had been in elementary school, Dad had gotten migraines so fierce that he'd had to shelter with the curtains drawn. "Black coffee is the crucifix to a migraine's vampire."

Sipping on zero-calorie sugar water, Char sat on her bed and opened her laptop. The mattress was barely thicker than double-ply toilet paper, but the room didn't have a desk or a workstation. This was a motel, not a five-star hotel.

She commented to herself, "That wifi, tho."

Her laptop synced right up at startling speed. Messages popped up everywhere. Jean Paul had emailed her, and WhatsApped her, and DM'd her on Twitter. He'd left five DMs since her last reply. The latest DM asked why she'd canceled "our" Netflix account. He didn't mention that he'd never pitched in for it, and that he'd insisted she upgrade to the multi-user account so he could have his own profile and watch list. He went on at length about how it was "reasonable" that he might need to watch his shows right now.

She closed Twitter.

One of her clients was a start-up looking to "disrupt" journalism that had come to her with a front page looking too much like the Washington Post to survive a lawsuit. Now they wanted to look like Reddit. It was a hilarious curveball, and she dove into potential designs. She could at least get them three drafts that wouldn't look like rip-offs.

Well, normally she could have done that. Somewhere during the second design, her eyes watered so badly the screen became an oily blur. Her forehead felt trapped in the grip of large hands, digging its thumbs into her temples. She tried rubbing the soreness away with the heels of her palms and it only made her head throb worse.

It was in her vision, too. Sun bursts snap-crackle-popped along the off-white stucco walls. Closing her eyes assuaged little. The sun bursts kept exploding against the dark backdrop of her eyelids for what felt like minutes.

When she opened her eyes again, streaks of violet and lime and raspberry splashed across the room. The walls, the dresser, and the carpet were all painted by the same visual hallucinations. For every streak, another searing fissure seemed open up along her skull. Was this what Dad had seen when he'd hid in his room with migraines?

Looking out her window was a mistake that left her whimpering. The sun bursts and colorful streaks intensified in the daylight. As much as they stung, they mesmerized her. There was a patch in the motel's backyard where every sun burst darkened, as though revealing the outlines of something healthy eyes couldn't see. The shape beneath those colors was puffy and wrinkled, like a cloud. She tried to make out more detail in the impossible aura tinged fog, and the cloud moved, as though to face her.

Then she threw up in the wastebasket.

She hid in the dark of the bathroom for the next hour with a damp towel over her eyes.

It was actually more than an hour before she could leave. It had to grow dim enough outside for her to not feel like she'd die if she saw another sunbeam. Once dusk brushed the treetops, she ambled outdoors, looking for Raleigh with the intent of buying as many pots of black coffee as he could carry.

Even in the dusk, she shielded her eyes. Sun bursts went off in her eyes with no bright light source. That brought the dread on that she'd finally inherited Dad's condition. If it was hereditary, why had it waited until she was twenty-eight to hit? The worst she'd felt prior to today had been brain freeze one summer at college when her dorm bought a snow cone machine.

"Raleigh?" she called, pushing open the door to the check-in and office. Arctic air conditioning blasted her in the face and she tottered backward.

He tilted his computer monitor away and rose to greet her. He had a feather duster in one hand. "Hey Char. Room clean enough?"

She tried resting one temple against the cool metal of the door frame. "I have a beast of a headache."

"Oh really? I've got a little convenience shop in the office. You like Tyenol, asprin, or ibuprofen?"

"Have you got any coffee?"

Raleigh rested the feather duster on his hip. "It's America, isn't it?"

An answer didn't readily come to mind. The pain kept grinding, like the lobes of her brain were rubbing together. She thought of those Greek myths where gods popped out of

people's heads.

Raleigh came closer, speaking too loud. "You don't look great. Stress headache?"

She whispered emphatically, tone urging him to quiet down, "Why would I have a stress headache?"

Bless him, Raleigh whispered his answer. "Your ex is being a prick, right? You were worked up enough that you moved out."

Thinking of Jean Paul made the brain grinding worse, and sun spots flared all over the parking lot. She could almost see the shape again, hovering over her car.

It was a lumpy cloud shape, or a brain shape. Clouds had lobes and wrinkled ridges like brains. This was like seeing the pulsing, burning sensation that filled her head, somehow projected across the motel. Like she was being stalked by her pain.

The cloud shape drifted across the parking lot. It was coming towards her, filling up her vision.

Raleigh said, "Charlotte?"

"Huh? Sure, Jean Paul's been pestering me a bit."

"So that's probably it. You're finally out of that relationship, and you're safe, and your body is catching up with you."

"I'd like to stop catching up with it, thank you. You said you have pills?"

"I got some PM ones that'll knock you right out. You'll feel like a new person in the morning."

Jean Paul woke her. It was her phone, buried somewhere in her shirt and buzzing like drunken hornets, but she knew

who the messages would be from.

She doom-scrolled through the texts until she lost her patience with the one in all caps. It read:

DO YOU WANT TO BE ALONE FOREVER?

She said, "Ass, I want to be alone right now."

As she blocked his number, the needles sank into her head. From the bridge of her nose to the back of her scalp, she was assaulted by a platoon of little pains. Her vision skewed, and it took her minutes to make out what time it was.

"2:12?" she said dubiously.

That couldn't be. It was daylight out.

It was daylight out because it was 2:12 in the afternoon. She had never slept this long in her adult life.

All night and no work? Her clients were going to lose their shit.

She grabbed her laptop off the floor. She must have kicked it off the bed last night. That grinding pain roared through her head as she opened it. It wouldn't connect to the wifi.

Swearing, she rose to carry the laptop to another corner and try connecting there. The mere change in height felt like it dropped an anvil on her. She choked a sob and held onto the bed frame to keep from falling. She slept for thirteen hours and didn't even beat the migraine? It was like it'd waited for her. She wanted to strangle it.

Sun bursts and streaks of colors that belonged only in children's crayons haunted her. It was thicker, painting the world in flashes. It weighed on her, making her feel like she'd sink through the floor.

It'd hadn't just waited. This was worse than yesterday. She thought of Dad lying still on his bed.

She had to get to a hospital.

The nightmare violets and rouges curved again, pop upon pop, giving the form of that two-lobed brain. It obscured her entire front door. She waded through it, and it felt as thick as billowing fog. Moisture clung to her clothes.

"R-Raleigh?" she called as she left her room.

There he was, face obscured by cherry red sun bursts. "Whoa, Charlotte. You look like you should sit down."

She sat down, face first. The gravel of the parking lot was cool, and as much as sharp ones stung, she wanted to leave them in her face. The temperature was an unsavory kind of relief against the pounding of her head.

The gravel around her creaked with footsteps. She tried to look up at Raleigh. All she could see was a shower of colors, and the curvature of an impossible mind.

She thought she hallucinated the feeling of warm clay in her hair. There was no clay in the motel. She didn't even like clay. It was so moist.

The air pulsed with the banging rhythm of the pain in her head, the pulse of the twitches rather than her heartbeat. It was like the world was telling her blood to fall in line. Orange sunlight beat down on her eyes, and then it was the cerulean of pre-fab swimming pools, and then the weary black of space photography.

She lay on a steep slope leading down towards a pond. Toads smaller than her toes hopped onto her jeans.

She'd driven past this place on her way to the motel. It looked smaller from the road. Amid the sun bursts and streaks of electric blue and powder orange, the pond's depths took an undeniably lobed shape. She was gazing into her own migraine. The misery that felt alien inside her was also outside her, those technicolor creases pulsing. This was herself outside herself.

"It's beautiful, isn't it?"

Char shrieked at the concept of the cloud talking to her.

It wasn't the cloud. It was Raleigh, with his gaudy bolo tie and long sleeves, standing beside her on the slope. He gestured a hand at the unmissable shape taking up the rest of her reality.

Char croaked out, "What?"

Raleigh put his hands on his hips, like Dad had done when she'd been petulant as a toddler. He said, "I didn't have many options, Charlotte. If you don't feed it, it comes for you."

She squeezed her eyes shut, not that it cut off the visions of that flashing cloud. The deep purples and the subterranean browns kept assaulting her.

But at least she didn't see Raleigh gloating. He went on, "You weren't my first choice. I really love you. You're a sister to me. It's that I'm running out of people. It was down to you and my literal sister. I'm going to have to lure her out here next, and she's a real headache."

It wasn't an option. Opening her eyes was an inevitability, to gaze upon the wiry image of her college bestie, chuckling over his shoulder at the flashing migraine cloud.

"Locals say it chose this place because --"

Char kicked him square in the balls. She drove her heel into his crotch until something popped and he squealed like agony evaporating into raw sound. He staggered from her, and into the flashing glaucous indigo and solar flare yellows and the purple of surfacing veins. For a second he was in-between the lobes themselves. Raleigh was reaching for her when he was sucked into the pond.

This was more than relief. No ecstasy had ever been as good as this nothingness. Her head was neutral - not a scintilla of pain in all of her thoughts. In that moment, she was sure that people underrated feeling nothing.

The flashing cloud of nonsense colors was gone. It left her on the shore of a tranquil pond, the tiny toad songs to entertain her. The clay was thick in her hair. The best shower of her life was ahead.

Also, her college bestie was gone. There wasn't a ripple in the pond to signify his existence.

Char might've felt conflicted, had her phone not buzzed. That buzzing made her wince for the pain that it would have caused her a minute ago.

A few flecks of blue-green drifted around the peripheries of her vision. Along with them, the dullest ache rose where the weight of her head rested on her neck. It was like a promise from something she couldn't see right now, that the migraine could blossom again.

Her phone buzzed again. It was Jean Paul. He had figured out a way to spoof a fake phone number in order to message her. He was begging her to "be reasonable" and "at least call me."

A call was out of the question. She gave him a simple text:

You can't give me space for two days?

Six seconds later, Jean Paul responded:

We. Need. To. Talk.

She weighed her phone between two pinkies, watching the neon green of glow sticks flit around the peripheries of her vision.

She answered:

In that case, I know where you can meet me.

GIVEN NAMES

LUCAS SHIPWRIGHT

The grizzled man behind the register squints down at you through his bifocals. As he rubs the folded-over fifty you gave him between his tobacco-stained fingers, the security thread catches the light. Hiram, you think his name is, though it's hard to say whether that's a nickname or what his mama stuck him with. His hair's been gray as long as you've known him; after being gone for over twenty years, yours has started to match.

"You look awful familiar," Maybe Hiram says, paper crinkling as he balls his hand into a loose fist. He puts his weight on it as he leans closer, inspecting your face. The rusted buckle loop of his bib overalls pops open, revealing a tanned and wrinkled tit. "You kin to the Stills?"

"Reckon I am," you say. "If I wasn't, Daddy did a good job of raising me to believe otherwise."

Hiram tilts his head and studies you longer. "Hard to tell

whose you are with that fuckin' diaper on your face."

You roll your eyes, but pull the N95 down until the nose wire rests beneath your bottom lip. One aisle over, you hear Zadie rifling through ancient bags of brittle and taffy.

"Well shit," Hiram eventually says, one side of his mouth creaking into a grin. "Never 'spected to see you 'round this way again, Wimple."

You jam your hands into your jacket pockets to discover a gum wrapper and yesterday's tissue. "Figured I oughta finally let the family meet my lady."

Hiram straightens up too fast, a clatter of popping joints. He glances toward Zadie, the top of her head visible over the shelves, curls red as a signal light and exactly as show-stopping. His eyes swivel in the opposite direction to study a Norman Rockwell calendar, and he nods to himself.

"Cuttin' it awful damn close," he grumbles, laying the fifty on the counter between you.

"Wasn't sure I was coming."

He huffs a laugh, but no longer smiles. "Yeah, you always were a selfish kid." Hiram pushes his namesake over with a flick of his nail. "You know damn well I ain't gonna charge you to get up the mountain, youngin'. Just get on with it."

You don't make Hiram repeat himself, though Zadie tries her best to make him take her money for the candy.

"Just nice to meet you, ma'am," Hiram tells her with a soft smile. "Be sure to tell Wimple's mama that I said hello now, y'hear?"

Zadie giggles the breathless way she always does when she's nervous, like the laughter shot up from the soles of her

feet and circumvented her lungs entirely. "Sure," she says, grabbing your elbow when you offer it, linking your arms together. "I can do that."

You pump the gas for her, then slide back into the passenger seat. Zadie's mask dangles from one earlobe as she fixes her lipstick in the rearview mirror. "What was that all about?" she asks as well as she can without moving her lips. "Did he clock me?"

"Nah, just me."

Zadie frowns; her baby pink nails click against the lipstick tube. "Why's it so nice to meet me?"

"Eh, well." You methodically tear holes in the tissue still in your pocket, hoping not to excavate your own spit in the process. "Y'know. Cis folks are weird like that."

"Yeah, but not usually that weird." She picks at a misapplied spot of pink just above the bow of her mouth. "I didn't dare use the bathroom after that rest stop at the border, but I guess it would've been alright."

"Need it now?" you ask, but Zadie shakes her head as she puts the cap back on the tube before tossing it into a cup holder. "Not far to Daddy's, anyway."

She turns the key in the ignition, then shifts it into reverse. As she looks in the side mirror, you stare past her, watching Hiram step into what might be the last phone booth in the state.

His eyes meet yours; Hiram nods and begins to dial.

"Bet he's only glad you ain't a lost tourist," you tell her, wishing you'd led with that first. Thinking on your feet has never been your forte. "But you're awful damn cute, so he

probably wouldn't have paid mind if you were."

Zadie sighs as she pulls the car back onto the road. "Delicious, home-grown mountain misogyny."

"Better'n phobia. Oh, and careful taking these curves," you remind her. "Roads're narrow, and ain't a guard rail to be seen up here."

"For someone who can't drive, you sure do a lot of wheel-grabbing," she teases.

"Why do I need to drive when I've got you, baby?"

"And what would you do if I couldn't drive?"

You shrug, watching the forest envelop the car again, clear blue sky disappearing behind the boughs. "Guess I'd just stay put."

Zadie laughs, her real one, the laugh she's only ever given you. "You're a goddamn mess, Robbie," she says, and you lean over to kiss the dimple on her cheek.

"Your mess," you murmur, finally undoing the snaps on your too-tight jacket. Six years with her, and you've still never loved another person more. The world could burn down around your ears, and as long as she was with you in the conflagration, it wouldn't matter. But there's more than the two of you now, you remind yourself, hand settling low over your belly.

The woods grow denser, but the branches know better than to scrape the finish from the car. Zadie keeps singing along to *Once More with Feeling*, and you don't take your eyes off of her light for the whole drive into the dark.

Daddy had greeted you both in his best shirt and slacks,

the same outfit he bid you farewell in when you left the mountain years ago. You made the tea, letting him and Zadie get to know each other, in the same kettle as your mother had. Her china cup, too, that you set in Zadie's hand, bone white with delicate golden flowers along the rim.

"He seems nice enough," Zadie offered later, once he'd gone up the trail to be with your mother for the night. "Didn't mean to give him my whole life story. Mostly, I was just relieved he had on more clothes than the guy at the gas station."

You kissed her goodnight, then curled up behind her in your childhood bed. Sleep gave you a wide berth, but she never knew, because you always wake up first anyway.

"Breakfast in bed," Zadie calls it, when you bring her the two pills that complete her. Before, she'd rifle around in her bedside table drawer to hand over your testosterone gel; for now, those days are gone, so she gives you her favorite lavender hand cream instead.)

The path up the mountain to your mother shows even fewer signs of age than your father's hands. Each painstakingly carved flight of dark stone stairs are as smooth and well-tended as they were when last you climbed them—only four, with the weight of the universe already draped around your neck. You hold your own hand now, listening to the girl of your childhood laugh and skip her way up. Behind you, Zadie huffs and puffs, new sneakers squeaking across each step.

"I did try to warn you," you say, and she grumbles a reply. "Glad you didn't wear those heels now, I bet."

"Well kill a girl for wanting to look nice for meeting her boyfriend's mom."

You turn at a landing and hold your hand out to her.

"Can't believe you didn't tell me your parents were separated–Jesus, but that was embarrassing. Almost as bad as not knowing you were Robbie Junior."

Her palm is warm against yours. "Not a junior," you explain. "Too many Roberts before me."

She rolls her eyes with an exasperated sigh. "Still could've mentioned about your folks before I flubbed it."

"They aren't separated though, is the thing, they're just… It's–It's complicated. You'll see."

Cell phones aren't good for much besides a flashlight on the mountain, and that's what you use yours as, the trees ever-thickening around you both. The grass fades away the further you climb; even the clay red dirt is little more than a memory.

Another step closer. Another. Another.

Zadie halts. "What happened to the birds?"

"Hmm?"

"It's not even like they stopped singing." Her fingers tremble where they've woven between your own. "They were tweeting loud as anything back at that tree," and she gestures back toward the silver maple you've passed. "It's like someone reached out and… I don't know, Robbie, just turned them all off."

You take in her face, the curl of her mouth as she frowns, the rapid movement of her rose-shadowed eyes as she listens for ambient noise. She doesn't seem to have noticed the silent breeze, making tree limbs shiver overhead without a single sound.

"They don't like anything else to be the center of attention," you tell her carefully, just as your mother told you. Zadie's hair is silken between your fingers as you tuck it behind her ear. "Pisses them right off not to be the prettiest girl at the party." The backs of your fingers brush her cheek, rosy from exertion. "And you're an awful pretty girl."

But Zadie won't be distracted so easily. "Who's they? Who's them?"

"Come and see," says the breath of the mountain from your lips.

Hesitation and fear war within Zadie's brown eyes, but her heart wins out. She loves you too much to turn back now, and you love her too much to let her run.

At the top of the last flight of stairs, you push aside the thorny vines for her—they sound like the wooden wind chimes from the dreams you've never told her about, an ancient echo far more melodious outside your skull. The sudden rush of sound overwhelms you with awe, even gratitude, that you could not only be allowed here, but welcomed.

You watch her Eve's apple bob as she swallows. "Robbie…" But Zadie says nothing more. Maybe your smile is convincing enough; maybe she hears a Call of her own. She joins you on the top step, and you walk into the sunlight together.

Zadie gasps, hand halfway to her mouth, then reaches toward an open, uncluttered sky. She takes half a step forward, then three more all at once, surrounded by the budding meadow, golden shoots breaking free from the ground to dare the sun's caress. Her eyes dart around, watching the little flowers spring to life at waist height, no longer a mere

painting on your mother's cup.

(You recall suddenly the night after your mother moved up here, how you flicked the rim of her teacup again and again, trying to recreate the symphony of the flowers. But time does not reverse for you. Not yet.)

She laughs like a song, head turning to find you. "It's beautiful!" Zadie shouts over the birthing din. "These look almost like some kind of myosotis," she says, lifting the head of a flower with a fingertip.

"What's that mean in English?"

"Sorry, scorpion grass."

You shrug.

"Forget-me-nots," Zadie tries again, and your eyebrows raise in comprehension. "Blame Linnaeus for the name."

"One of your coworkers at the arboretum?"

"God, if only."

You smile and point past her, as excited as you are dreadfull, and she follows your gaze in time to see the first moth break free from the heart of a flower. It flits to a neighboring bloom, and then there are two, four, sixteen, dozens of iridescent wings casting prisms in the sunlight, painting her face a thousand shades of brilliance.

"Oh my god, Robbie." Her voice is a stunned whisper. "What are they?"

"Some things in the mountains are older'n God," you tell her. "Best not to go around namin' things what ain't yours to name."

"You're really gonna tell a biologist not to name something?"

"Not some thing. Just this one in particular."

Zadie shakes her head, grinning again as a tiny moth perches on her finger. "If you say so, Mr. Stills, but someone has to have named these little guys. The flowers, too."

"Two parts of the same critter," you explain. "They only bloom and burst once every thirty years, and they only do it here." Zadie brings the moth closer to her face, tilting her finger in the light to watch the burst of color from its wings. She giggles as its thin antennae brush her nose, and you feel this morning's pancakes churn in your stomach. "Ain't nobody alive what lives off the mountain ever seen them but you."

A trio alights on her wrist, a gossamer bracelet. "This is starting to get ridiculous," says Zadie. "I feel like some fucking animated princess. Like a goddamn fairy tale."

"I won't tell Murdoch if you won't," and she snorts with laughter.

"Speaking of old folks, where're yours?"

"I'll go fetch them in a minute." Tall stems part for your feet as you walk toward her. You don't dare let yourself blink, lest you miss even a moment of Zadie, now, a princess in her own court, an unknowing goddess in her own right. Moths perch up and down her arms as you carefully reach up to cradle her face between your palms. You kiss her as deeply as you dare. Something like a sob tries to bully its way out of your throat as the side of her perfect nose settles into the notch of your crooked nostril.

Instead, you swallow it down, and promise her, "I'll be right back."

You've never been in Mother's House before. This was never a place meant for you to see, not in your current capacity. The stone walls are higher than they should be, given that you climbed down through the old stump to get here. Rows upon rows of chrysalis line the walls, glowing synchronously, like fireflies in a glass jar, making shadows dance along the floor as they expand and contract.

Daddy's knelt in the same place every host before him has kneeled, too, the smooth rock of the floor polished and eroded from centuries of reverence. He opens his eyes, and smiles tiredly up at you as he takes your hands between his.

"Never thought you'd come back," he says quietly. "Thought maybe you'd forgotten, or else didn't care."

"I wasn't gonna," you admit.

A rustling stirs up from the oldest row. It feels like being screamed at, like chastisement of the highest degree.

Daddy murmurs to them in a language you won't know for a few minutes more, and they settle themselves. "What changed your mind?"

You chew at your lip before answering. "Curiosity," you say. "But als–" You shake your head, and place the palms of his hands against your belly.

He blinks several times. You can tell immediately when he's understood, more elation in his eyes than you've ever seen.

"My beautiful daughter," he says, and you wince, but Daddy continues. "My perfect son. Glorious creature–what a miracle you are!"

You both reach to wipe each other's eyes at the same

time, and Daddy laughs. It's a sound you haven't heard since the day your mother moved. Sure, you did plenty to make him laugh as a child, but not like this. Not the one he reserved just for her.

"Do you know why my Margaret named you Wimple?"

"No, sir."

He rubs your stomach beneath your navel. "When she had her quickening, she got mad," and his eyes crinkle in delight, "because you gave her the wimpiest little nothin' of a kick! And she looked down and said, 'Now I ain't gonna raise no Wimple.'" He gives your stomach a parting pat. "You know how it is, with giving names. Sometimes they just stick, even if they're wrong."

"You think she's mad now that I'm only another Robert?"

"Oh baby, no." Daddy squeezes your hands. "You don't know just how damn proud she is, but you will."

He releases you again and reaches for the pouch at his belt. "I don't think I can do this," you tell him in a rush. "What if it doesn't work this time, and then I'm all alone?"

Daddy's shoulders shake. "You're askin' the right questions, boy. You belong." He holds it out on his palms for you to take, brightly polished silver gleaming in the light of the chrysalises. "It's time," Daddy tells you. "They ain't gonna wait forever."

You look down at the tool in your hands. "I thought it would be bigger," you say, and Daddy chuckles.

"Yeah," he says as you gingerly ease to your knees in front of him.

"Yeah, you'll be just fine," and his fingers seize on your

face as you drive the scythe home through his carotid and yank down.

Daddy's still smiling as the blade draws through his ribs. You remember him telling you once that, "You'd best marry an outsider who knows how to gut a pig, because I ain't gonna teach him." Instead, you all-but-married a vegetarian. Zadie would be vomiting down here in the near-dark if she had to feel the hot rain of blood against her skin and hear the squelch of guts as you search within the hallowed walls of Daddy's abdomen.

Once she'd found her stomach again, Zadie would probably be able to marvel at an appendix in full use. You can almost hear her critiquing the unnecessary mess you've made, but they never passed down the art of laparoscopy. They only gave your ancestors the scythe and the urgent demand to be fed at regular intervals, lest they rise and glut themselves.

You pluck the golden chrysalis from where it lies fastened to Daddy's appendix. You're covered in gore, but as soon as you've hung it in place beside the rest, the blood and viscera turn into dust. Looking back, you watch Daddy's body be assumed into the floor, not even a drop of blood left to be seen. Only the black pouch he wore remains, because it is no longer his burden, but yours.

Mama twinkles where you've put her, like a star, shining brighter than all the rest.

Maybe it makes you a coward, but you're glad to have missed all the screaming. You still wake some nights hearing the echoes of Mama's in your ears. Part of you wonders what

Zadie's sounded like, if it was more rollercoaster than haunted house.

By the time you emerge from the stump, the flowers have disappeared again. What was once a lush meadow full of life is now barren; the sweet floral perfume has given way to the stench of rotting straw.

All that's left is the moths, and Zadie. Her body has crumpled and caved in on itself, the moths breaking it down to the correct size slowly as they spin their gold. She only whimpers now, her voice faded to a mere soft monotone, but her eyes find yours.

You sigh, wringing your hands, and sit down beside her. "I tried so hard not to fall in love with you. So goddamn hard." You watch another strand of red hair get tucked into the weaving web. "And then, when I couldn't stop that, I figured, well. The world sucks anyway. I just won't go home. I'll let them come and eat and end it all." Zadie's ears are nearly subsumed into the sides of her face now, eyes comically large as the moths work their way up.

You almost want to laugh. Almost.

"But then…" You frame your hands around your abdomen, the way Zadie had the day you told her she would be a mother. "It might have been a fun adventure, traipsing around with you at the end of the world. But that ain't no way to raise a baby."

"Could," croaks Zadie. A long laborious series of breaths. "Told."

"Didn't know how." You want to apologize, but you don't.

Silence falls between you both, only the quiet hum of the moths as they work and the rhythmic crunching of bone. The

sun is high in the sky, and you're thirsty, but you won't leave her. Zadie won't face the beginning alone.

"I swore I'd keep you safe," you say at last, "that I'd protect all of us." The name of the mountain feels false on your tongue when you say it in the speech of every host that came before. It's the first time you've known it had a name, at all. But there's no translation, so you tell Zadie, "Here, on the mountain, is the safest place in the whole fuckin' world. Ain't nothin' or nobody can separate us now except time."

Zadie tries to speak again for hours. The sun is beginning its descent when you finally hear her whisper, "Lonomia." You watch as her lips disappear behind silk forever, and the moths converge on her head to beat it down to size.

It's not a word you've ever heard before, but Zadie knew lots of things you didn't. As the moon rises and you take Zadie into your mouth for the last time, you think it might make a beautiful name for your daughter.

SAFE FOOD

XOCHILT AVILA

"Dinner is served."

With a wet, heavy *thump*, Cedar's takeout drops onto the table, still wrapped in a thin plastic bag soaked with condensation. Towering above, their father seethes, his wide shoulders blocking the kitchen light before moving to collapse in his seat. He easily opens his bag, whereas Cedar struggles, their bony fingers weakly tugging on the double-tight knot. Residual oil clings to their skin. Greasy. Sticky. *Unclean.* But washing their hands will come off as "lollygagging," so instead, they towel their fingers off inside their hoodie. The old man has groused about it twice since coming home, and he does again before grabbing his fork.

"S'too hot to be wearing a sweater. Wouldn't have to be embarrassed about what you look like if you'd just fuckin' eat."

Cedar ignores his quip and abandons the knot, opting to tear straight through the soggy film to excavate their dinner.

Shiny, red oil stains the styrofoam, and a pungent spice wafts out from its lips. They can already feel it burning the inside of their mouth. Hunger bangs within their stomach like a church bell for mass, but the thought of a single bite drowns them in nausea. Of course, their father knows this. He knows all the best ways to make them suffer.

"Stop fucking around, *Jamie*." He smiles around each slow syllable of their long-deceased name, filling the space between them with the sour stench of his breath. "*Eat.*"

Cedar forces their trembling hands to steady as they open the box, their eyes immediately assaulted by smoldering heat. Red enchiladas, their *father's* favorite, from one of their few dining options in rural Maryland. The whole plate is buried beneath a mountain of chili flakes, and a rancid, dark grease has seeped down into the corners of the container. Everything their palette venomously rejects. Everything they've *begged* him not to bring home.

"Dad, I can't eat this."

"You're going to eat it. *Now*," the old man warns, exasperated. "I swear, you never acted this way with your mother."

"Mom actually listened to me!"

Life hadn't been easy when their mother was alive, but she did everything she could to shield Cedar from her husband's wrath. She'd made life something worth living, something more than a constant battle just to be heard. "Mom actually *cared* about me."

"It's not my job to care about you. It's my job to *keep you alive*." Their father's chair topples behind him as he stands.

"And you're clearly trying to make me fail at it."

A massive hand snatches a fistful of Cedar's dark, brittle hair. Searing pain rips across their tender scalp, but his grip is too strong to pull away from. "You think we can afford for you to be picky? I'm sick of it. Sick of you pretendin' there's something *wrong* with you. You used to eat what she made. Now you're gonna eat what I tell you to."

Suddenly they're falling face-first into their dinner. Scorching mush floods into their nostrils, some reaching their clamped mouth and eyes. Cedar screams against their teeth as it burns them, sharp as a blade, but they can only squirm uselessly against his hold. It does nothing but lacquer their face in the agonizing mess and make their father cackle.

"Eat it. *Eat it!*"

He rubs their face in it until they're sputtering, body falling slack from exertion. Only then does he let go. A crimson streak smears across the table as they slide off, collapsing onto the filthy linoleum. Cedar cries and coughs until they spew out yellow bile. Above, they hear the click of a lighter and a disappointed growl.

"Clean up the mess you made."

Tobacco lingers in the air as their father meanders off to smoke and drink the night away. Cedar remains where they are, eyes still shut tight. Everything hurts, but for now, he's gone, and that's worth relishing. Somehow, eventually, they find the strength to drag themself to the sink and wash away as much of the filth as they can. For hours after, Cedar's skin flares with needling pain, but the monster doesn't emerge from his den. And that feels safe enough.

Gilded in warmth from the attic's sunbeams, Cedar presses the book against their solar plexus and breathes. Sandalwood and sage hug the air, no doubt from their mother's possessions. This is where their father hid it all away after her heart attack. The last echoes of her time on earth stowed away in haphazardly stacked boxes.

He hates it when they sneak up here, and he'll make his anger known if they're caught. Downstairs, they can hear the slamming of cabinets, and the low hum of conservative talk radio. Noise is another one of his favorite weapons against Cedar, and still being on workman's comp means he can wield it constantly. Their waking hours are filled with it, but distance and the fluff of insulation help dull the sharpness of the chaos below. Even in death, their mother finds ways to protect them.

"Thanks, mom."

Cedar admires this current piece of her collection; A plum-colored, leatherbound edition of *The Adventures of Sherlock Holmes*. Reading had been one of their favorite pastimes together. Their mother, like them, enjoyed the tranquility of silence. Her fragile heart meant she couldn't take young Cedar to the park, couldn't chase them up the jungle gym like the other parents. But that suited them just fine. They would snuggle together, basking in the afterschool sunlight as they read stories. At least until their father came stomping home demanding dinner.

Cedar can't recall if they ever read *this* book together, but they can easily imagine it: her perfect hands, red polished nails thumbing through the weathered pages. Like a treasure

box, they ease it open, mindful not to bend it too harshly. Dust springs out into the air, and they inhale it freely before burrowing their nose into the ancient paper.

Their withered stomach barks with desperate hunger.

Nearly half the pages are gone now, neatly torn down to the spine. Cedar strums their finger along the feathery edges left behind before ripping out another. They break the paper into little bits, then place each scrap upon their tongue until saliva saturates it into a woody pump. It goes down smooth, and they repeat the motion again and again, basking in the fleeting satiation. They know it won't fill their sunken cheeks or narrow thighs, but it brings them fullness. It brings them close to their mother again. And so, they feed.

The next evening, Cedar tries their hand at true sustenance.

Like a cautious deer, they ease down the wheezing staircase to the living room. Creaks are plentiful in their ancient home, and while Cedar is usually a master of this descent, they're also running on fumes, brain foggy from days deprived of nutrition. It makes their movements sloppy, and though they do their best, they hit at least three squeaky boards before reaching the bottom. They listen. Waiting.

Muffled screams and explosions echo from within their father's chamber, probably from one of his war documentaries. This means he's probably still awake and, given the hour, absolutely plastered. Cedar remains as diligent as their brain allows. His rage is already on a hair trigger when sober. They do their absolute best to avoid it when he's drunk.

Through the kitchen doorway and across the living room, they can see the cabinets. If cautious, they can make their way over and scrounge whatever they can stomach from the pantry. Even if it's just a cold can of beans, they'll take it. Their stomach *begs* for it.

Progress is slower through the living room than it was down the stairs, which deepens their anxiety. Though adjusted to the dark, Cedar's eyes swim with famished haze, darkening the edges of their vision and everything within it. Including the nearby coffee table. Panic bites with daggered fangs as their foot collides against a wooden leg.

Fuck.

A sharp scrape echoes through the home as the table slides across the floor. It isn't a long noise, but it's loud and immediately chased by a lull from the bedroom. He's coming. Cedar quickly squirrels into the nearby closet. Stuffed with moth-bitten winter coats, it's a narrow fit, but they're small enough to sit snugly on the floor. But the sagging door doesn't close behind them. It probably hasn't since they were in diapers. Cedar pulls it in by the knob as far as it'll go, leaving a small but unmistakable gap. They can't move now. They can already hear his befuddled shuffle down the hall.

Heartbeat pulsing in their neck, Cedar waits, the bastard's crawl agonizingly slow. It takes nearly a minute before he finally waddles past the door, face flushed pink in a boozy glaze. He moves into the kitchen without a single glance down. From within, Cedar hears the soft gasp of the fridge, then the clink of glass, and soon enough, they watch him meander back with two beers in tow.

Cedar doesn't breathe again until his door clicks shut, and they don't emerge from their hiding for several minutes longer. Acrid liquor lingers in the air. It emboldens the young prisoner to finally make their move to the kitchen pantry. Cautiously, they open the door.

Though dark, they can make out the boxes in the pantry, long and caked with rust, and every single one padlocked. Tackle boxes from the garbage, the ones their father hadn't touched in years, Cedar had thought. A stained napkin with a scribbled note sits on top of one.

SINCE YOU LIKE TO WASTE FOOD, I'LL MAKE SURE THIS STUFF STAYS NICE AND SAFE UNTIL YOU LEARN TO APPRECIATE WHAT I GIVE YOU.

Cedar's stomach wails in ravenous fury. They search the rest of the cabinets, but not a single can or crumb can be found. Teeth gnash on chapped lips until copper seeps onto their tongue, kindling their hunger further. But there's nothing they can find here. Cedar stumbles out through the backyard door and into the midnight air. There, they find their mother's rose bushes, and finally they crumble and quietly weep.

Hours pass as Cedar lingers in the garden. They admire the bloomed roses, so shiny and red. Eventually, they locate their mother's old pruning shears, plucked from a nearby terracotta pot. With hands shakier than they'd like for such a deed, they snip one of the flowers halfway down the stem, mindful to keep enough leaves for the next flush.

Of course, they learned that from their mother. Gardening had been another escape, particularly when the weather warmed and beckoned them to nature's sanctuary. Cedar can still wear their childhood gloves, and in fact, they fit with an uneasy looseness, particularly around their slight wrists. An unpleasant sight.

Cedar looks to the flower instead. Gleams of moonlight kiss the supple petals with a gentle glow. They bury their nose in the center of the blossom and inhale long and deep. It smells like home. It smells like safety. Wetness prickles their eyes dark with shadow and early crow's feet. Without hesitation, they sink their teeth into the spongy bulb. Floral sweetness assaults their palette, eliciting a starving growl as they gnaw through it like a carnival apple. Cedar savors every bite, even knowing their father could step outside any moment for a smoke.

They spy the book when they reach in for their second bite, tucked far back in the thorny bush, packaged in a thick layer of plastic wrap. Cedar gasps, reaching in without concern for the thorns that rip their sleeve and scratch their arm. Dirt clots and tiny pill bugs roll off the surface as they bring it out into the open. A quick glance assures their father is still in the house, giving them the confidence to unwrap their prize.

They hold a well-loved copy of John Steinbeck's *Grapes of Wrath*. The cover is worn, and its pages fray from past water damage. Cedar sees the tip of a much newer envelope poking out from the top, surprised by the heft and thickness of it. Excitement bubbles in their chest as they pull open the flap.

Money. *A lot* of money.

A cursory glance reveals more cash than they've held in their life, far more than they feel comfortable counting in the open, even in the safety of darkness. There's also a letter, its penmanship neat and heartbreakingly nostalgic.

Cedar,

I hope that's the name you still go by, but know I'd cherish any name that you've chosen. Know that you, Cedar, are cherished. I pray you'll never have to read this letter. Hopefully, we'll use this money together and escape this place. But I know you'll find it if that doesn't happen. Every day I fear I've seen my last sunrise. So, I've saved every dollar I can. Forgive me, I've taken money from your birthday cards. I've sold some of our favorite books. I've done other things, too, things I'm not proud of.

Use this money. Get out. Your father made me keep my parents at arm's length, but we've got family up in Penn. They'll take you in without question. Be strong, and take care of yourself, because the world won't take care of you. It doesn't take care for people like us. It doesn't care if we live or die. So, care for the little child who made me feel so seen. Tend to them like a garden.

And please, don't forget to eat.

Mom

Several days pass before Cedar is ready, the prospect of freedom pushing them onward. It blunts their father's insufferable sounds and even wills them to swallow down the few foul meals he bothers to bring home. The bitter

curmudgeon doesn't comment on it, but it seems to soften his anger a degree. Cedar has never been so riddled with terror, yet they sleep better than any week since their mother passed.

Cedar owns very little they can't freely abandon. It's choosing amongst their mother's belongings that rips their heart in two. They accept they'll have to leave the rose bushes behind, so they settle for a single pressed flower, hoping its scent will carry on through their travels. The books are harder to choose from, but they narrow it down to some of her favorites, ones they haven't devoured in their sickly habits.

Sooner than not, the night to depart arrives.

Time approaches the edge of dawn when Cedar finally eases out from their room, backpack slung across a shoulder. Familiar sounds of *Fox News* vibrate from their father's bedroom. Good. Once more, they make their slow crawl down the narrow hall toward the wooden stairs. A walk they've made countless times and never will again.

They can do it.

They *know* they can do it.

Or they would, if not for the imposing figure waiting for them at the bottom. Their father flashes a hungry smile, and Cedar feels their blood run cold. "Thought you'd been actin' queer lately. What're you doing up so late, Jamie?"

Cedar remains frozen at the top of the stairs, but for once, they don't shrink away. They don't run to hide in the garden or the confines of their mind. "It's Cedar, and I'm leaving."

He lets out a cruel little laugh, the steps groaning beneath

his massive boots as he begins to climb. "Oh, are you now?" Cedar can already smell the liquor on his lips. It bounces off him in waves, engulfing their nose in its bitter sting.

"How you're planning to do that? Last I checked, *I'm* the only one who makes money 'round here. What're you gonna do, walk out into the street and hope for the best?"

Cedar takes a step back, and he takes another forward.

"You ain't stupid. Lazy, a crybaby, sure, but you ain't *dumb*. You got some kinda plan?"

Cedar can practically feel the cash stowed away in their backpack. With one good yank, he could snatch it all away. In his eyes they find a frightening sharpness, even through the drunken haze. It shakes them. Instinctively, they look away toward photos that decorate the stairwell wall. Straight at the only remaining portrait of their mother.

Their father grins wider.

"She's helping you, huh?"

"I don't have a fucking plan, *I'm just leaving*." Cedar snaps as strongly as they can. "You're sick of me being here, so, I'm sparing you the trouble. So just let me go."

"She can't help you, kid. Couldn't even help herself." The old man shakes his head, shortening the distance with yet another step. He could reach out at any moment and drag them down. "She was a weak, sad woman. Always complainin' about her heart. Could barely keep the house clean or food on the table. And then she made you *soft*."

"She was doing her best! After everything you put her through, it's no wonder she died. It's *your fault!*"

"Everything I put her through? It was her *goddamn job*."

In a flurry, the space between them finally closes, the drunk's grip like iron on the front of Cedar's shirt. Withered cotton rides up and displays their gaunt form, cavernous stomach and ribs jutting out from their pale, bruised skin. "And YOUR JOB is to LISTEN TO ME!"

"GET AWAY FROM ME!"

Cedar shoves him away, drunk off adrenaline and the siege of decades' worth of silent anger. Small as they are, it's just enough to push him off the step. Gravity does the rest. This time, they don't avoid his gaze, bloodshot and astonished, before his body tumbles backwards.

A sickening crack engulfs every other sound in the house when his head hits the floor. The right-wing radio trash, the ancient wheezes of the house, their own gasping breath. It consumes it all. Slowly, Cedar follows, unconsciously moving at their usual slow pace. Once down, they check his vitals with the same lack of urgency. They already know the answer. It's given away by the dark lake that seeps out beneath his skull.

Cedar is keenly aware of how this appears. They scan every window in sight, but the dusty curtains are drawn, and it's the dead of night on the eastern shore of Maryland. The nearest house is at least a quarter mile away. No one could have heard their confrontation, and nobody cares enough about their father to inquire about his well-being. They'll remain undisturbed for a good long while.

They are truly alone. There's nothing stopping their departure now, but for the first time since afternoons with their mother, the house is quiet. Or nearly so. Quickly, they hurry to their father's bedroom. Putrid rot fills the air,

permeating from mountains of beer bottles and moldy fast food bags. Cedar only stays long enough to rip the stereo's cord out of the wall. Finally, silence. Pure and serene.

Cedar eagerly returns to the living room. Not even the presence of the corpse can spoil their happiness. Eyes flutter shut as they listen to the natural sounds of their childhood home. It's so beautiful, and for a long while, they're content to just breathe in its rhythm.

Until their stomach growls once more.

Eventually, they have to act. But calling the cops is out of the question. There's a good chance they'll be blamed, and that's reason enough to deal with the bastard alone. Cedar studies the massive cadaver, painfully aware of how it dwarfs their malnourished frame. They look at their hands, as frail and starved as the rest of them.

How can they deal with this all alone?

The answer comes easily. Surprisingly, it doesn't stir an ounce of repulsion. Why should it, given everything he's robbed them of? Their mother, their dignity, their life. Plus, they can't remember the last time he's done a grocery run. Surely there's plenty of space in the old deep freezer. And he wanted them to get their strength back, after all. Their mouth floods with saliva as they begin the unclean work.

Cedar decides to take a sample before dealing with the rest. It's nearing sunrise, and the gnawing in their gullet is now constant. Carving knives are easy to find, left untouched in the kitchen drawers. And, of course, their mother's shears. It doesn't matter if blood seeps onto the floor. They have all the time in the world to tidy after.

Now they just need to eat.

It's harder work than anticipated, and far from elegant, but they manage to carve a hunk of wet, glistening thigh meat. Cedar considers all the ways they can prepare it. Perhaps they'll fish out one of their mother's cookbooks and some of the spices abandoned in the cabinets. But first, they need a taste. They need to feed. They need to erase every shred of him from this world.

The flesh is far from tender. It's quite chewy, in fact, with a slight metallic tang, but for the most part, surprisingly mild. Not at all unpleasant. Cedar smiles, the redness clinging to their trembling lips, and swallows it all.

THE THING THAT LIVES IN THE HOUSE

NEXUS HOPE

Dear Beatrice,

I miss the quiet. I do not think paint should yell. I do not think drywall should shout. And yet, in the winding halls of this home, the dark and rusting light fixtures scream, the floorboards squeal, and my voice is reduced to nothing in comparison.

Despite the loss of your presence, I never feel truly alone. The windows are always gossiping and they say the most terrible things. They tell me of the neighbors' marriage and the feud between the wallpaper and molding. The tables groan and complain. *My legs hurt,* they cry. *Go bother the counters,* they moan. The dining chairs comment on my weight and the ones in the living room sweetly ask me to stay forever. They say they are lonely, but how can they be? When I know that they talk to the throw pillows behind my back. When I know that they have an ongoing argument with the bricks of the fireplace.

I want to be alone in the house, Bea. But the rugs have a scratchy personality and the furniture coddles those who find themselves there. The bed murmurs sweet nothings in the ears of whoever is unfortunate enough to fall into its plush blankets and mountainous pillows. I try not to listen, but as I lay awake at night, I can hear the rumors the chandeliers spread and the soft waxy sobs of the candles when they find out they're about them.

This place is mine, despite your best efforts. When people knock on my whining door, I answer with open arms, and an inviting smile. They look at me with equal parts surprise, excitement, and something else that simmers in the back of their eyes and lies in the tightened corners of their mouths. The kitchen stove chants the evening menu and I can almost remember what it tastes like. My guests never seem to hear until their throats are red and raw from the blades the burners put in their food for laughs. I can hear the floorboards chatter about the quality of the guest's shoes. *This style is dreadful,* one board says to the other, *went out of fashion years ago.*

The houses lining my street judge my leaking roof and my dying flower beds. The people in them judge me too. Those

other houses. The ones I cannot hear but I feel as if they should scream. This house that took me, my pride and my death, is charming in ways I cannot explain. Its siding tells the most engaging stories and the windows are lined by shutters that share my sense of humor. It's odd. I know my home is feared. I know I am feared. The house and I have become one in the minds of the people outside. We became a curse, a haunt. It is unfair, Bea. How could they be the ones that are victims of this place when the moment I opened the door I was swallowed by its decaying walls? It is unfair. They think I am terrifying but I am terrified. How can they possibly assume that the house they hate would somehow favor me? I wasn't chosen. I wasn't anything. I was naïve and my will was weak. I did not listen to those I loved. This house did not pick me. I am just like any of my visitors except something went so very wrong, and now, I can always feel the warm trickle of blood from my ears.

Bea, I want to say I regret my actions, but I cannot. I will not lie to the dead and the dying. Of all the guests I have hosted, not one has been loud. Their clothing does not weep and their shoes do not cackle. My body aches for that silence and that is why I must invite them in. Please, you must understand, it is a part of my nature. The quiet they bring does not keep for long, but it is sweet while it lasts. I do not wish ill on those who come here, but no matter the cost, I must keep them before the grass once again becomes just as talkative as it is dead.

Bea, I ask that you do not respond to this letter. I do not know what I would do if your words came on paper that did not whistle, written in ink that did not choke. Something has happened to me. Something terrible and loud. Something that

makes me listen to skin and hum over the sounds of teeth. I cannot imagine what I might do if your knock on my door was silent. If it did not come with its own sound to add to the ruckus. I know you believe in my ability to be stronger than the noise, but I am not. I am weak. So very weak. And the moment I realize your pearls do not speak at length of the weather, you will be any other guest. A poor visitor in my home. I will do anything for that quiet, Darling. Even though I know it will be swallowed by my orchestra.

I remember that your face was lovely, or at least I thought so. I remember the way the trees would rustle when we walked. The birds would sing their little tune and the breeze ruffled your brown hair. Or, no? Was it red? I can't seem to recall the color of your eyes or the sound of your laugh, but I know I loved them. I loved them almost as much as I long for that elusive quiet. I regret not telling you when I had a voice of my own. A voice I did not share with the drapes and the tiles. I remember that you warned me against this house. I no longer know what you said, but you knew. Somehow you knew that this place would wrap its fingers gently around my arms and dig its nails in. My hands, now. My nails. You were right not to come here. Not to visit. Not yet.

I miss you, but not nearly as much as I miss the lack of sound. When I say this, Beatrice, take every word to heart: If you knock on my door, I will listen for your blood singing ballads and I will wait for your nails to squeal their obscenities. They will not, no matter how desperately I wish they might. I will open my door and I will invite you in, maybe hug you and bury my face in your silent hair. If you walk through the threshold of

my hell, I will keep you here, Bea. I do not want you to stay, but I will keep you. I know I will. I will keep you within these walls until your eyes start to scream and your bones start to laugh.

Do not come here. Even if I ask. It has taken everything I have to ward you away knowing that your tongue would not squeak. That your cheeks would not whisper familiar lullabies to keep me awake. Lullabies that would make my eyelids heavy and my head fuzzy with sleep before this change. Before I forgot the words. Before I forgot your voice and what melody means. Believe me when I say that I will take you. I do not know what happens to those I take. I believe that they might die. I hope they do. But sometimes I can hear their voices coming from the plants in the corners or the paintings on the wall.

You are the only one who I feel I can speak to, but even then it is a challenge. I know I loved and trusted you but I can't recall why. How can you long for something you never knew? Because I do. Everyday. I wonder if you would sound more like the blankets or the pillows. Maybe you sound different altogether. Maybe your voice would be sweet and silent and mine for the taking. I can barely feel myself anymore, Bea. Feel my arms or legs. They are stiff like wood and my joints are nailed together. I do not know where the house ends and I begin. I can reach out and touch the wall but all I feel is my own hand on my skin.

Bea, I am no longer myself. I am the monster that lives in this house. Its hulking wooden frame whispers me secrets I wish I did not know. If this horrid song ever ceases, I will find you, but I will be broken beyond repair. I will click my teeth to fill the empty space and I will scream between sentences. I will miss our untainted moments. Moments in which I didn't have to think about the opinions of the lamp or the lectures from the books living on the shelves. Moments when I knew if your hair was brown or red.

I will miss the way you looked at me during that time and I will miss being able to move my face in reciprocation. To pull up the corners of my mouth without thought, to squeeze my eyes shut with joy. I ask you to forget what I was before the noise. This cacophonous racket that has taken my mind. I promise to miss you just enough.

With all my love,
The Thing That Lives in the House

SO, THIS IS FREEDOM?

STEVE NEAL

Years of neglect and abuse had plunged the bathroom into an irreparable state of disrepair. Every night, at the beginning of his shift, Henry took a mop to it, and replaced the stench of stale piss with a nostril-burning cocktail of chemicals. Old grime clung to the grout and tiles in hardened peaks; immovable, as much of a fixture of the gas station as the dull lighting and stale hot dogs.

The mirror was the cleanest thing in the room, only clouded in the corners where the reflective material wore away with age. As always, he showed it extra care, refusing to let the last glimmer in the gas station fade on his watch.

Despite his attentiveness, it never showed him an attractive portrait of himself, the one that haunted smudged memories of distant lands. Now, skin so pale it appeared wan beneath halogen lights looked back at him. Thin, black hair framed his jaw and fell over bulging veins in his neck that seemed to writhe and pulse beneath his skin. A trick of the odd lighting.

He feigned a smile; The one he flashed at customer's inappropriate comments and repetitive jokes. His lips cracked and flaked as they turned upward, exposing teeth that looked white enough, at a glance. "Remember, you're in charge. This is your world. Your reality. Take back control, and create the world you want around you. You are God." The learned mantra from last week's therapy session fell comfortably across his tongue.

There was no immediate burst of joy, no spark of excitement for the hours ahead. Like every other night, his head drooped towards the floor as he wheeled the mop and bucket out of the bathroom.

Change came in the subtle form of a single decision, minutes after he took his seat behind the bulletproof glass at the register. For once, he didn't slip into a mental void, staring at a nondescript point on the shelving between the chips and protein bars. Instead, he took a ream of receipt paper and started to doodle, letting his hand guide the ballpoint pen as it glided across sheer white edges and crafted a city skyline emerging from the bottom edge. There was a familiar comfort to it; the embrace of nostalgia, the calm he'd found in halcyon years surrounded by watercolors and stained overalls. To a time when he wasn't beleaguered by wayward thoughts and grisly ideations.

Such was his captivation, he didn't look up when the door chimed nor did he notice the growing irritation radiating from the side of his neck.

2:01.

Green digits on the cash register dragged a smile across his face. He'd made it through the worst part of his shift. No more college kids stumbling through the aisles, clinking with arms full of booze, or staring endlessly at snack options through bloodshot eyes. He'd hear fewer derogatory comments or snickers between groups, and catch fewer people looking over their shoulders as their hands dipped into coat pockets. For the rest of the night, it'd only be the regulars; the odd night-folk of the town. Those with set routines and obsessive specificity in cigarette brands and scratch cards. People who had little desire to converse, content to let him drift inside a world of his own control, created in black and blue ink.

It worked. A simple mantra to keep his mind quiet, to veer his life back onto a path he could control. He looked down at the receipt paper and the scrawled buildings and hints of still life inside their windows and on their streets.

"I am God," he said.

A brush of air tickled the small hairs inside his ear as if someone whispered to him from inches away. A shiver ran down his spine, sending goose pimples rippling across flesh, and a tautness to his gut that quickly changed to nausea. He felt the vomit rising from his stomach, surging up through his esophagus. Both hands clasped over his mouth as he sprinted

across the store, bursting into the bathroom as vomit slipped past his fingers and sprayed across the porcelain bowl. He heaved multiple times until not even bile passed over his lips.

Out of breath and weak to his toes, he dragged himself to a stand and hovered over the sink. Handfuls of water swished around his mouth before he spat them down into the drain. The acrid funk didn't leave, embedded in the crevices between crooked teeth.

The mirror showed an even more pitiful depiction than usual. Sweat glued hair across his forehead and down the sides of his face. His skin was both thinner and paler, exacerbating every slight blemish on his face. Locked onto the glassy, sunken eyes that stared back at him, he figured it couldn't hurt to try again.

"This'll pass. You're in charge. This is your world. Your reality— "

A shimmer of movement stole his train of thought. Something among the ends of his hair, a faint shadow that slithered across his collarbone. He swatted at himself, hopping to the side to get what he assumed was a bug off him and stop it from crawling down his shirt. After a flurry of slaps, he checked the mirror, looking at every possible angle of his body. No squashed corpse or splattered blood stained his skin—All he saw   were pulsing veins running down the side of his neck, past his collarbone to his sternum, sinuous paths that split and merged like tangled underbrush.

"Remember, you're in charge. This is your world. Your reality. Take back control, and create the world you want around you. You. Are. God."

"Didn't know Carey was letting y'all come in hungover these days. Or hell, maybe you're still half-drunk." Something resembling a hacking fit and a laugh cut him off. "Shit, two packs of Marlboro Reds."

Henry had a faint recollection of the man's face, but there was nothing unique about him. Easy enough to mistake for any of the countless other middle-aged men with leathery skin and salt and pepper stubble. But he'd remember him now. The Jackass.

"Fourteen fifty-nine, please." He slapped the pair onto the counter.

"Damn. Y'all robbing folks in here," the man said as he fumbled with his wallet.

"I don't set the fucking prices." Henry bit the inside of the lip. He hadn't meant to say that. It was just a stray thought that slipped out unconsciously.

The Jackass sneered at him. "Fucking mouth on you. Don't you know it ain't safe for people like you round here?"

Henry tapped the customer-facing screen on the register, afraid to attempt to say anything else for what might spill out.

The Jackass grumbled further insults under his breath as he scanned his card and punched numbers into the keypad. Once it went through, Henry slid the packs into the small metal valley beneath the bulletproof glass with a flick of the finger.

"Have a great night," Henry used his usual customer service voice, airier and a few notes higher than his regular

speaking voice.

The Jackass flipped him the bird as he stomped out over old linoleum and barged through the door into the dull lights of the parking lot. Henry watched him the entire way as he packed the cigarettes against an open palm, thrusting the cardboard into his skin with an impotent rage. He walked beyond the gas pumps and over the road, where he dissipated among the shadows. Faint ghosts existed in the darkness, the warped reflections of the store's interior on the glass. Henry caught a glimpse of himself, hunched and sneering, neck veins reaching up onto his cheeks and across his forehead. The sight caused him to fix his posture, standing up straight and stiff. Both hands clasped the sides of his neck, expecting to feel hard ridges against his palms, but his skin was smooth, void of the protrusions he'd seen in the reflection.

Henry looked back at the spot on the glass and saw the reflection he was used to: the pasty, tired boy who ran from his problems.

Solace returned in the form of his makeshift easel and the collection of colored pens he scavenged from behind the counter.

At no point did he stop to consider what the next building would be or how the sprawling neighborhood would form together. It flowed freely from the recesses of his mind, pulled from vague memories of childhood naivety. No buildings grazed the underbelly of clouds or darkened the sky with plumes of smog. Stray dogs didn't prowl the streets and growl at midnight passersby. When he filled in windows, giving full

lives to imaginary homemakers, no one slept on a couch until they were back on their feet, and furtive bugs didn't scurry at the hum of electricity. People sat at tables and dined with loved ones, tiny smiles on their faces. Warmth radiated from windows and spilled onto the streets with a subtle wash of orange across cobblestones. No one slowed in their cars to holler at people on the sidewalk, no one side-eyed those who looked different. Those tacit inquiries and distrust didn't exist. People just belonged.

When he tried to turn and pull himself away from the incessant scrawling, and focus on one of the many untouched tasks around the gas station, he never made it beyond the twist of his hip. His feet always remained in position; knees locked forward. For the first time in recent memory, an honest solution existed before him; how dare he attempt to walk away from such revelations? He'd known it all along. How tangible a better future could be, if only he'd found the courage to remove the mask of conformity that kept his gaze low and voice timid. If he stopped trying to gain their acceptance as something he wasn't, how simpler life could be. No more second-guessing every response to make sure it fits in with cultural expectations. All he had to do was exist in his truest form, as he'd been born. Be the God of his own doing.

Finally content with the unearthed revelations of his created world, Henry went to step away from his post at the register. Again, his feet remained rooted to the ground, knees stiff and forward, but there was no rotation in his hips, nor any flexibility in his abdomen. A rigidity emanated upward, spreading across his chest and to his shoulders, and down both arms until the pen trembled in his hand. Warm air caressed his inner ear once more, but this time unimaginable syllables broadcast into his ear like lips pressed against his eardrum; a ceaseless, nonsensical murmuring. He wanted to struggle, to call for help, but could only stand there, doodling across his canvas.

At times he choked, his throat closing. Others he felt vomit rise and fall. Worst of all was the pain. Across various points on his body, it felt like something burrowed inside of him; penetrating through muscle fibers, and winding itself around his bones. He wanted to scream, to beg for mercy but his body was not under his control. Maybe if he focused on the movements of his hand scrawling across the paper, further creation might rid him of whatever bond froze his muscles in place.

The bell above the door chimed as a woman in her mid-thirties strode in, face bundled beneath the thick coils of a woven scarf. She offered a sideways glance and stifled a chuckle at his stiff, terror-emblazoned appearance. As she poked around the aisles, he stared at the faint reflection of himself in the bulletproof glass. The reflection warped his face, turned it into a carnival maze's approximation locked into an eternal staring contest with itself.

"Y'all have any Bagel Bites?" The woman shouted from the back row of freezers.

Henry had to fight to shake his head less than an inch, a battle that felt like his vertebrae would pop and fall from the column. Sparked pain so great that tears blurred his vision and welled against his bottom eyelid. In the haze beyond his

tears, beyond the twisted visage of his own face, he saw the woman stomping down the center aisle, past the motor oil and pain relievers.

Small movements refocused his gaze on his reflection. At first, he thought them to be strange refractions of light, twisted by the glass's construction, but as his eyes trained back in on himself, he saw there was no mirage. They sprouted from every orifice on his face. Tiny seedlings wriggled and emerged from his tear ducts and nostrils, sliding out over cracked lips. He felt none of them, assuming the stiffness across his entire body numbed him to their growth,

"*I said*," she slapped her hands down onto the counter. "Don't y'all have any Bagel Bites?"

He fought against his seized muscles to shake his head again, a timid back and forth that he wasn't sure would be perceptible. A subtle movement caused the shoots to grow further in the reflection, writhing in the air like vines searching for something to anchor themselves to.

"Oh, I didn't realize you couldn't—I'm so sorry, I wasn't trying to be insensitive or—Sorry, sorry," she backed away from the counter, hands raised, exiting the convenience store without breaking eye contact.

"Are you… God?" The voice was his, raspy and strained, but the words were not.

Control returned to his body as the woman scurried across the parking lot. Both hands inspected his face, ready to yank and pull at the weeds that sprouted from inside of him. He felt nothing unusual, not even an errant hair he could blame the mirage on. The stretched image of himself he saw in

the bulletproof glass didn't look so odd anymore and *certainly* didn't contain any protrusions.

The cramp in his right hand became more prominent with each passing second until the agony of it screamed at him to pay attention. It brought his gaze down to the sprawling city on the paper that he'd obsessively scratched on while transfixed on his reflection. Thick lines coiled across every building's facade, the ends reaching up towards the sky. Others burst from between the cobblestones and pavement. Not an inch of his creation remained unsullied. A mass of vines infected all of it.

Henry walked out from behind the counter, a shuffle moving him through the aisles towards the back of the store.

"What the fuck is happening to me?" He muttered.

In the reflection of freezers at the back, his flesh was covered in fissures, pulled apart by escaping vines and twigs.

"I am." The words came from his mouth, but this time it was not his voice. Something more guttural. Hisses and pops like radio interference muddied the vocalizations.

Both of Henry's arms wrapped around his head as he fell into a squat. "Stop. Please stop."

He kept his eyes closed, afraid to catch even a glimpse of himself in his periphery. Nowhere was safe. A sliver of glass or polished metal existed in every crevice, ready to show him a deformed, forgotten version of himself. But outside, in the parking lot he could stare at the sky, wait until sunrise. Looking through his eyelashes, so the store remained blurred and indistinct, Henry crept through the aisle and toward the door.

Through the filter of his eyelashes, he could see the light in the store, the vague edges of end caps, but there was solely darkness outside the glass. No fluorescent downpour from above the gas pumps, no vague colors from the myriad signs, not even the dull amber cones of streetlights. Not a single guiding light to beckon him to safety. It had to be a trick of the eyes. A consequence of squinting, surely.

A foot away from the door, Henry stood, arms outstretched ready to push the door open and sprint to safety. But he had to check. A flick of his eyelids was fast enough to avoid focusing on his reflection standing across from him, but enough to see only darkness lay beyond the door. There was no outage. No fuzzy shapes swimming in shadow or buildings glimmering with the silver of unabated moonlight. A solid wall of black, like vandals had painted the storefront glass in the few moments he hid.

It prompted a second look. Longer. More vulnerable.

In the reflection of the pitch black, the store was empty. No shelves or magazine racks, no walls, or refrigerators, not even the scuffed tile flooring. It was only him. As he knew himself. Plain and unassuming.

"What are you?" He asked.

"I am God." His mouth chattered, the words a perfect mimicry of those he'd uttered earlier in the night.

Henry ripped himself away from the door, and focused on the packs of gum and candies that lined the customer's side of the counter. "You're in charge. This is your world—"

The cacophony of shattering glass caused him to throw himself to the floor. He winced, expecting an onslaught of

agony as shards rained down, slicing and puncturing his flesh. Like hail on a tin roof, they clanged against the tile and shelving as they fell from the air. Henry tensed further, but the pain never came. Only when quiet returned did he uncover his head and dare to peer beyond his arms. The metal frames the windows sat in were gone; swallowed by an encroaching darkness that billowed inward like a morning fog. The perfect nothing engulfed the street and gas pumps unhindered, enveloping magazine racks as it poured over the walls and onto the tiles.

Henry scrambled to his feet, darting through the aisles and into the bathroom. He locked the door behind him as if a metal latch could stop the flood of darkness. Huddled against the far wall, his eyes stared unblinking at the door. The familiar, pungent scent of chemical cleaners caused his eyes to water, but he couldn't break sight. Tears fell onto his cheeks, eyes strained to a squint.

Beyond, chaos reigned; a roaring arose like a hurricane tore through the aisles and ripped shelving and goods apart before the abyss sucked them inside. The door shook, rattling in its frame, seconds away from flying off its hinges—when he blinked, the sound receded.

In its place, soft wisps of darkness crept beneath the door, trickling into the room, swallowing slivers of the room in its listless invasion. Henry struggled to pull his shirt over his head and stuff it against the gap at the door's base. Before he could shove it into position, he saw the wriggling on his bare chest. Right below his collarbone, a charcoal seedling sprouted and swayed in his periphery, dozens of them in various states of emergence. Some pushed against the inside of his skin, bubbling his pores as they pushed through. Others were inches long, spiraling and swaying as they searched the air.

Panic thrust him to his feet, facing the mirror. The sprouts were everywhere. On his shoulders, ribs, hips, all over his back, behind his ears. With his tongue, he could feel them on the inside of his cheeks and running along his gums. Blood pooled in his mouth for each that broke through.

"Who is God?" No more static clouded the words. Clarity returned but not control.

"Please, stop. You are God. I'm not. Just, please leave me alone."

The darkness from beneath the door had crept up and consumed it entirely,   spilling forth into the room and taking over the tiles and toilet, until he stood in a void, only the mirror and the smiling reflection of himself remaining.

"You pitiful thing. This time, this place, these luxuries you no longer want. The betrayal you've shown this body. Be true to yourself, to me. Let me in and I will show your true face to the world. Just take it off. Remove that facade and show the world who I am, who you are. Or shall I take it by force?"

"I don't want any of this. I didn't mean it."

"There's no need for pretense anymore. Act not the blubbering fool in front of me, but the survivor you are. I offer you a choice, God. Give or take? Stand tall or stand back? Which one of us leads?"

The stalks grew into meandering limbs that encircled his body, covering most of his exposed flesh so only chunks

of pallid skin shone through beneath. They writhed and pulsated, muscles that twitched and tensed as the charred vines dragged themselves out further from his pores. A living thing, slowly taking control of him.

"Me. I'll do it. I'll give you this. It's yours."

With his words, the mirror cracked, and spiderweb fissures raced across the glass   fracturing his reflection into many. He felt the rigidity return, the loss of control that froze him in place rise faster this time, unabated.

"It will hurt less this way."

All he could do was watch his body act under something else's volition, trapped inside, frozen behind his eyes, every movement shown to him in the many reflections of the mirror. His hand reached out, pulling one of the larger shards of glass from the mirror. Blood spilled from his palm and trickled down the fragment from the tightness of the grip. His arm raised; the point driven into the crown of his scalp. With ragged jerks, he pulled the shard of glass down his forehead, along the bridge of his nose, and over his lips and chin. A deep cut that split the skin down to the bone. He inserted the shard's point down the side of his nose and pushed the glass inside, between cheekbone and torn flesh. He began to saw.

Skin flapped free, loosening around his eye socket, deforming his lips into a downward sag. Henry watched, helpless, as he repeated the action on the other side. With his face barely clinging onto his skull, the being dropped the glass and reached up with both hands. Fingers curled inside the wound and pulled, tearing flesh away in solid chunks, letting it fall to the floor in wrinkled heaps. Beneath it all, a

mess of stygian branches and roots pushed itself forward and emerged from the remnants of his crumpled body.

"Now, we are free. Now, we are God," he said as he reached for the door.

THE MASK IT WEARS

SARAH MUSNICKY

Be silent. Be small. Be still. The next scare is just around the corner, and you must prepare.

There's a routine to the art of a scare. First, get into position. Second, wait for the first round of screams heading in your direction. Between the soundtrack, the clanking of metal bars, and the slamming of walls, it is easy to get distracted. Not you. You've always zeroed in on what's important – giving the customers what they paid for.

They've paid for a show.

Get back to your list. Be ready. What's next? Third, you get set up. This year, your spot is in a cell, but the bars are wide enough to squeeze your body quickly through with no problems. You're meant to play the part of a victim this year. Your task is to scream, to beg for people to come save you, but none of them can. Not without threat from other actors tailing close behind. You have two black sheets set up flush against the wall, out of the sight of patrons but easily accessible to you. Popping in and out, there are multiple ways for you to hunt guests down.

That doesn't mean the guests can't find their way in. There have already been a couple of incidents this season where you've had to get out of dodge fast. Too many drinks and guests tend to get a wee bit adventurous. They don't pay enough for that kind of exploration.

No, they need to come into your section, where you can promptly scare them and keep them moving through, in and out, lickety-split. A conveyor belt of motion, there's a routine. You always abide by the routine. It's what keeps you going on nights when the guests decide to drink some extra douche canoe juice.

Tonight is one of those nights.

You slink back through the bars. The metal catches at your ribs, but you don't register the ache. It'll kick in once you wake up in the morning, and your muscles are all stiff. In the cell, you hug the darkest corner, arms outstretched against the wall, and wait like the predator you imagine yourself to be.

Time is like the slow-steady drip of water coming out of a faucet. It hangs in the air suspended. Waiting for something, the faintest wisp of fear fluttering in someone's heart.

Until you hear it, the desperate pitter-patter of feet

running up the halls to the right of your room. High-pitched screeches are nearly overpowered by the pounding thrum of the maze's musical score.

Before you have the chance to move, a couple of women sprint past your cell, still screaming. They don't see you. No one ever sees you. You like it that way. What you don't like is not getting the chance to pop out. But hey, when people are that freaked out, it's best just to conserve energy.

The soundtrack lulls you into a trance, leaving you almost senseless until a banging at the cell bars finally connects with your brain. You peek out from the shadows with steady feet and see your coworker, Chuck. His eyes are wild and frantic, and his hands are beating at the bars. Blood drips down his forehead, but you can't tell if it's the makeup or real. The fake scratches all over his face make it tricky to guess.

A tingling sensation at the base of your skull warns you this is not routine. The pattern is broken. The train's off the track. He's saying words to you, but it's all static against the thrumming of bass echoing against the steel walls of your room.

You get closer until you're nearly nose-to-nose. Adrenaline, an electric slap to your insides, ignites when he grabs the front of your thermal and pulls you in. He looks behind you and back again, watching for something, someone.

You hear something crash just outside, and a high-pitched whine reverberates outward. You both grab your ears to shield yourselves from the mind-splitting sound before the noise cuts out. The ambient music is gone. There's nothing but the sounds of your breathing, and Chuck's before terror

returns to his face.

"Fuck, man. Get outta here. Go! Go! Go!"

It doesn't click until you hear casual, slow footsteps down the hall. Without the soundtrack to cover them, you can hear everything. The speed of the walking, coupled with Chuck's fear, gives you a pause. What the hell is going on?

The footsteps get closer, and Chuck jumps like a rabbit. With one more glance at you, he bails, running away from whatever danger he thinks is coming. This isn't the routine, but it could still be nothing. It wouldn't be the first time you'd had an overly invested customer cause havoc.

The question of "What if?" lingers in the air. There's always an exception, and it is the exception that proves most difficult to grasp. You decide to do what comes naturally. Stick with the routine. Be silent. Be small. Be still.

You get back into the shadowy corners of your cell and wait. This time, something has made its way under your skin. It's an invasion of discomfort. Your skin feels tight, nearly bursting, swelling and expanding, and aching to be popped. Fear. You're feeling fear. How gross.

And then it steps into your room. You hear it on the other side of the curtain you typically go through to get into position at the start of the night. You've always imagined when facing a predator that it would breathe heavily, but that's not the case here. It is still and waiting. The space between you two is too close for comfort. Pinpricks of sweat form, bubbling up at the top of your scalp as your blood pressure rises.

You almost gasp when it moves again. A slow, steady step-step as it takes in the space of your room. There's not

much. Metal walls and a chair opposite the cell, a chair that has distracted many customers too foolish to realize what lies waiting when they take a seat.

It looms into view, but you don't move. The person is tall but moves smoothly. The awkwardness that comes from the height has been ironed out with time. A mask, one of the ones sold at the stalls outside, is stretched across their face. The base is white with a stretched-out devil's grin of a smile. An unremarkable basic design. The only splash of color is red streaking across the eyes toward the mouth in what looks like a handprint.

It is then you take notice of the knife in their hand. You look for a colored zip tie to confirm its authenticity. When you notice the absence of one, you realize Chuck had the right idea. You should have gotten out of there when you had the chance.

It moves over to the chair and turns it to face the cell. Sitting down, the masked figure looks directly at your corner, and you're caught between the mental space of 'fuck a duck' and 'what's next?' You both stare until it starts to play around with its knife. An intimidation tactic.

"It's no fun if you keep hiding in the dark," he says. A smooth baritone that would be riddled with temptation if the fucker wasn't holding an actual weapon. Stabbing isn't your thing. Your corner is growing claustrophobic, and decisions have to be made. Wait for the guy to come kill you, or at least pop out and show yourself.

"Fuck me." You push off from the corner and move to the center of the cell to stare. It isn't the type of show you

normally give. Frankly, just standing there staring isn't enough to entice anyone. But you do. Trying to ignore the knife and the slow, imposing tentacles of dread trying to worm their way through your stomach.

It happens in seconds. Pushing the chair back, a couple of strides to the cell closes the distance before he reaches his arms through the cell bars to get at you. You leap back, but considering his build, you know there is no time to waste. He can get in easily. With no goodbye, you turn your back and sprint towards one of the curtains against the wall. Lifting it up, you push through and start walking quickly.

Secret corridors are built to make it easier for actors to get to their maze spots. It also makes it easier to get to the front of the maze in case of emergencies. This is an emergency.

Tight and narrow, you scramble forward desperately to get to the next section. You need to warn the others ahead. A crash against plywood behind you is your tell. He is coming fast. You continue to move in the dark until you reach an opening at the end. With the grace befitting a drunken pigeon, you barrel out and pivot to move further into the maze. The maze music is still blaring in this section. Speakers are still intact.

Of course, you could make a loop and return to your section. You could ignore everyone else and go back to hiding in the dark, hoping everything will resume as planned. Coulda woulda shoulda.

It doesn't matter. Just move.

You pass by wooden boxes covered in blood. Fake body

parts are strewn about, but you take no notice. You're looking for the next performer, Max's, spot. You just can't remember if she's hiding about in the corridor coming up on the right or if it's past the wall of hanging bodies after that.

The screeching sound of metal clashing against wood echoes behind you, and you make the mistake of looking back. The man, hulking and brutal, is striding behind you, knife in hand, carving like a cliché against the wooden frame of a poorly constructed opening. Yeah, the fucker is enjoying this.

Making a right, you try to look ahead to see the ghost white, blonde bobbing head that'd indicate Max is there. But you can't see shit. The shadows are particularly mocking. Turning the tables on you for all the scares you've racked up now that the position is reversed.

"Max! Where the fuck are you?" The music squashes your attempts to yell, and you realize if you get caught now, no one will be able to hear you. "Fuck, fuck, fuck, fuck, fuck." Panic sets in, and your legs begin pumping. At this point, it is just time to get out.

You move past the bunkbeds, mindless, thoughtless, until you smack face-first into a hanging body. A solid mass, you bounce off and land flat on your butt. Getting up, you push your way through, just focusing on the pathway ahead.

A hand grabs you by the hair and yanks you back. You shriek girlishly high and lash out to grab one of the bodies for leverage. A flash of movement cuts down towards your right arm. You barely register the sting of the blade as your fingers contact the mattress-like cushion dangling from the ceiling.

You kick back with your left foot hard over and over until you feel the fingers release from your scalp. Liquid trickles down your forearm, and the coppery scent brings home the reality. You're bleeding. This isn't a game or a simulation. This shit is real. Go.

One after the other, you push aside the bodies until you're back into an open, clear path. Run. Go. Forward. Faster.

You know where the other corridors are, but he is following. You can't lead him down those in case there's a possible evacuation. So, you take the main hallways. They come one after another. Pop-up animatronics, strobing lights, and manufactured screams, but you pay no mind.

If you could get to the end, the supervisor on standby could lock the guy in. You'd be safe. Things would go back to normal. The routine could be re-established.

Just as you enter a room full of pulsating flashes of shadow and light, something hits you hard from behind, crashing you to the floor. Your chin makes contact, and the taste of blood fills your mouth. Like a frightened animal, you try to scurry away from the crushing weight, but greedy hands force you over until your eyes are directly locked with his.

This close, you can see his gaze. The mask that hides his face can't hide the laughter in his eyes, and that sends a surge of anger up your spine. Before he pins down your hands, you reach up for his plastic mask. He punches out, solid mass colliding with your cheek just seconds after ripping off his feeble cool-bro disguise.

What you see is just ordinary. There's nothing meaningful about this stranger's face, and that makes the situation more

frustrating. He's a generic white guy who would be considered respectable and forgivable in the '70s or '80s. You'd hoped that whoever was trying to kill you would at least be hot.

Instead, he punches you again, sparking black dots to pepper your vision. You lay on the floor and barely register his face closing in on yours until his lips are right against your ear. "Now it's your turn. Let's see what you've got under there."

Before you have a chance to connect the dots, he jabs downward with his knife. Your chin jerks back, absorbing the impact, but something catches. You try to move away but are caught. Eyes widening, realization dawns. Then his hand begins to saw away at the thin, fragile flesh.

Too soon. This can't be forced. You aren't ready.

Your fingernails scratch, desperate and angry against the assailant's face. Knife undaunting, he continues his task with a wry smile. Warm liquid trickles and then pours thick as the threads are sliced. Nerve endings sing their gleeful screams as hungry metal strips your face bare. Cool numbness settles in. Shock. Thoughts collide but fail to stick. Too soon. Yet, like an automaton, you continue to bat away, growing feebler with each swat of your hands until the final thread attaching your face to the tissue beneath gets cut. It slides off, flapping slightly as if in protest before he picks it off you like sad bologna.

You lay there on the dirty floor, lights still pulsing on and off, shadows coming in and drawing back with each lightbulb burst. Cold starts to seize your limbs. The nerve endings feel like electric fire, starting out like a spark before catching flame. Blood pours out hot, creating an unpleasant contrast with the slow tumbling freeze trying to take hold.

A bark of laughter rings over your head as the man holds up the face into the pulsing light. He hasn't bothered to look at the gleaming mass that is underneath. He isn't noticing what has been so rudely awakened by the forced removal. Instead, with the prize in hand, he stands up and turns. You hear pants rustling. The sliding movement of the knife being wiped clean on the fabric. Nothing will clean up the mess you're about to make of him.

The mask is off now.

A surge forces your body upward. You ignore blood, sweat, and pain that bursts with each movement of your legs as you take your shaky feet and push upward. You stride forward, one, two, three, before touching his shoulder. Forcing yourself on tiptoe, you push your true face as close to his ear as you can and utter your final words for the night:

"You haven't seen what's underneath yet."

He turns to look, knife in hand, and he sees you in that flashing dance of shadows and light. He sees the real you.

The squirming, pulsating mass of spiraling flesh unfurls itself from the cavity of your skull. Terror, his, peppers the air, tasting of cheap cologne and cloves. Before he can run, your hands lock down on his shoulders and press. He must see what he's done.

As the last vestiges of humanity leave you, you flash a lipless smile before opening wide, revealing the rostrum deep in the dark that will rend his flesh apart. Tentacles splay and wrap around his head, bringing you closer still. Mania, giggly and hot and sweet, takes hold as he screams, screams,

screams high and scared, and finally free.

Tentacles close in to end his screams forever. There's a squish. Skulls are fragile and break more easily than plywood. Fragments get caught in the fleshy underside, but it's nothing. He's nothing, not even worth the effort to feed on, and it is easily brushed off.

His body grows limp, and you drop it to the ground. Adrenaline starts to wind down, and you can feel the fatigue from all his bullshit start to crash. None of this needed to happen. Then again, it never does.

You squat down and take his lifeless hand in yours and take note of the face he took from you. Tan threads hang feebly onto the skin, but they're still present. That'll make reattaching much easier when you get home, but you'll have to assess the damage in better lighting.

Standing up, you decide to return to your original position. In the dark and quiet of your corner, if the maze supervisor needs to find you for questioning, they'll know where to find you. No need to be near the body. Just keep it simple. Be silent. Be small. Be still. And everything will go back to the routine there was before.

BITEMARK BITCH

OLIVE J. KELLEY

BITEMARK BUTCHER IS CAUGHT: WOULD-BE VICTIM SLAYS KILLER

July 6th, 2021

The man allegedly responsible for thirteen near-identical murders in the metro Denver area has been identified as 61-year-old James Theaker. The Aurora native was killed on Saturday, July 2nd, after attempting to enter a young woman's house. According to police reports, when he tried to pin the woman to her bed, she killed him with a blow to the head. The woman was sent to the hospital when emergency services arrived, and she has since been released from treatment.

Local and federal officials held a press conference this morning to comment on the matter. They confirmed that the DNA found at six crime scenes matches that of James Theaker and, while their official investigation will continue to gather evidence, they are "99.9% certain" he was responsible for the rest.

The woman who brought the Bitemark Butcher to justice refused to comment and will not be named in this publication.

COMMENTS (6)

StephenR64: *Glad he was caught. Grateful for the boys in blue who always keep us safe out here.*

butterflyqueen98: *Informative as always! Thank you, Denver Post!*

rubiesred: *RELEASE HER NAME! TELL THE WORLD WHO KILLED HIM!! PUT HER TO TRIAL!!!!*

(more)

December 29, 2021

The day Anya Shaw's charges were dropped was supposed to be the first day of the rest of her life, but instead, as she stepped out of the courthouse in a gray woolen coat, she felt as if it had already ended. She smoothed her hand over a red, angry scar: the perfect impression of a man's teeth on her throat.

The sky is dark. It's going to snow later, she thought.

Anya pulled her phone out of her pocket and pressed play on her music as she walked to the bus stop. With the black knit cap pulled over her auburn hair and her thick-rimmed

glasses pushed up her nose, she looked much like anyone else on the Denver streets. The reporters' eyes glazed past her. Photographers lowered their lenses. All was as it should be, the same as six months ago.

The trial was quick. Proving that James Theaker killed those women was easy; convincing the jury that Anya had no other choice was what dragged the trial out. Theaker's DNA was on almost every crime scene, including tufts of his hair glued with rust blood to the ball peen hammer that claimed his life. The bag he left on Anya's floor was just as damning.

One (1) duffel bag, New Balance, with a brown stain on the interior handle.

Contents of bag:
One (1) length of rope, length six feet four inches
One (1) rag, soaked in chloroform
One (1) black balaclava
Two (2) black New Balance shoes, size 11
One (1) crowbar
One (1) knife, blade measuring eight inches

Despite this, and the 99.99% DNA match, the jury still took nearly seven hours to deliberate, leaving Anya in a state of apathetic anticipation for even longer. As soon as she was validated in her use of deadly force, she left.

Theaker found his victims on the bus, yet there Anya was, standing in the center row between all the occupied seats. A man beside her glanced at her chest. A woman two seats forward met her eyes before looking away, darting her gaze back to her phone. A baby a few rows back began to cry.

A figure standing in front of Anya turned to face her. Brown eyes, hair firetruck-red. She opened her mouth and even through the noise canceling headphones, even through the riot of music in her ears, Anya knew what she said.

"Anya Shaw.".

The bus stopped. The rear door between them opened, and a group of harried people pushed past Anya to exit.

By the time the doors shut again, the woman was gone.

Anya arrived home to a still, empty apartment. After James Theaker broke into her home, every moment of peace was antagonizing, agonizing. Quiet meant danger; silence meant death. When he gagged her, she was quiet—when she slung the hammer into his skull and turned him into a rotten stain, he was silent.

Even her blood-soaked mattress had been taken by a clean-up crew. Anya paid for the service herself but she swore she still smelled the coppery rust of viscera on her skin. Shards of bone splintered her sheets, dry skin caked under her crooked-cut fingernails.

Now, after arriving home with the trial still lingering in her head, her apartment was quiet, until it wasn't.

It was quiet, until a dank, rotting scent crept under her nose.

It was quiet, until Anya's head hit the floor, and everything went silent.

"Anya Shaw."

Red hair. Pale skin. The bump in the night—a bus seat in the sweaty afternoon.

Her doppelganger.

"You," Anya said. Her vision cleared. She was tied to her bed with four lengths of rope.

Again.

She didn't bother to struggle this time.

"Hello, Anya."

"You know me," Anya said. Her voice was deadpan. It often was. "I don't know you, though." The woman took a step closer, emerging from the darkness at the foot of Anya's bed. "You know me better than you think," the woman said. Her eyes glittered like beetles in the darkness. "You killed the love of my life."

Anya's mouth twitched. "I see."

The woman's face convulsed and her lip spluttered. "That's all you have to say? That's all he's worth?" she spat through barely restrained rage. Even Anya, historically inept at reading subtle emotions, felt the horror radiating off this woman.

Anya remained silent.

"He saw you on that bastard bus, with your silky hair and legs for days. He saw you, and he decided he wanted you. What about you was so special? What about you made him overlook me, done up just as he likes his women, for you? You–" She gestured around the apartment. "You bare-faced, psychopathic fucking freak."

"Untie me and I'll show you what he saw in me."

The woman tilted her head back and laughed. "Good fucking try, bitch," she sneered and paced along the width of Anya's bed. "He wanted you, and you killed him. You–You fucking–" Her words morphed into a violent snarl and she rushed to the side of Anya's bed. Up close, Anya could see her moles, her freckles; her green eyes flecked with shining brown, evidence of life in an otherwise dying, pallid face.

She dug her too-long nails into Anya's hair and yanked. The touch was a perfect mirror of Theaker's, Anya knew– her muscle memory wouldn't soon forget the touch of the man who helped her be reborn. However, with this woman's sharp acrylics and smooth palms, it felt different. Anya barely chanced a breath.

"You took him from me," the woman whispered. Her breath smelled of decay.

"Are you intending to kill me in return?" Anya responded. "Don't you want to see how it felt?"

"I could have been everything to him," she said, ignoring Anya's question entirely. A drop of spit fell onto Anya's cheek. "Ruby Theaker, his partner in crime. I would've shown him, I would've convinced him."

"If you're a killer," Anya responded simply, "then kill."

Ruby's face went nearly gleeful with Anya's permission. She retreated, leaving Anya prone on the bed, and walked over to the corner of the room. Ruby picked up a small duffel, her back turned to Anya. When she stepped over to the bed again, she held two items.

One (1) duffel bag, New Balance, with a brown stain on

the interior handle.

One (1) knife, blade measuring eight inches.

She held the knife reverently, laid flat in one palm. It couldn't be Theakers blade—that was surely locked away in some evidence closet watched by the careless pigs who handcuffed Anya to their car, still covered in blood— but she regarded it just as fondly.

"Ruby," Anya said, finality leaking into her voice. "There's something you don't know."

Ruby ignored her and grasped the knife in both hands, raising it high above her head. It conjured an image in Anya's mind, a recollection of an old film, backlit and thunderous, and in that moment, she twisted her wrist out of the poorly tied knots.

In one inhale, she slashed her hand across the thick air between them and stole the knife. Ruby's acrylics might've been something James Theaker liked in his women, but they made for clumsy knot-tying.

On the exhale, Anya slammed the smooth pommel of a never-used knife into Ruby's temple.

Ruby woke to thick darkness and loops of rope secure around her wrists. Still, she yanked on the restraints, just as all the women did before.

Anya's voice came from the darkness, the only sensory input in a muted world. "You know, you might not've been my type before, but I'm starting to see the appeal."

"Fuck you," Ruby spat. "Let me go."

"You came here to kill me, and now you're making

demands," Anya murmured, barely an inch from Ruby's ear. "Didn't you want the whole experience? The Bitemark Butcher special? I'll even tell you the one thing you had wrong about him, the reason he never went for you."

In an instant, the blindfold was ripped away. Anya stood, still dressed in her clothes from court, with her blouse's sleeves rolled halfway up her arms, bunched at the elbow. Her copper hair shone in the dim light and her eyes– brown, Ruby thought– gleamed gold, or maybe yellow, like a snake about to strike.

"You were always James Theaker's type." Anya crossed her arms. Her biceps were firmer than Ruby might've expected, toned and clearly quite strong, if the thrumming behind her eyes had anything to say about it. "You just weren't mine."

"What the fuck does that mean?" Ruby managed. Fear gripped her as Anya came close again, leaning down and dragging the pointed tip of her nose up Ruby's jaw.

"Your perfume," Anya said. Her lips brushed Ruby's pulse, just where Anya's was scarred red. "It's strong."

"You're psychotic," Ruby whispered.

"Again," Anya murmured, "you came here to kill me, Ruby. I understand the urge. I do have the blood of thirteen women on my hands. Just don't pretend we aren't the same, don't feel the same… Urges."

She bit Ruby's throat. Ruby cried out– really, she attempted to scream, but instead let out a long, choked-off moan. Anya's teeth were sharp and her jaw was strong and Ruby felt the skin begin to tear under the woman's sharp incisors.

"Fuck," Ruby gasped and yanked at her restraints until Anya retreated. Her jaw dripped with fresh blood. When she smiled, red coated her teeth. "You're insane."

"You like it," Anya said outright, and the truth sat hot between Ruby's traitorous thighs. "You wanted him to kill you, didn't you? You want me to kill you? You want to kill me? Either way, you want blood. Am I correct?"

"No, no, no," Ruby whispered. "No, you're wrong."

"I'm not." Anya adjusted her sleeves until they sat above her elbows. She climbed onto the bed and swung one leg over Ruby's waist, tied at all four limbs, straddling her with the knife held in one hand. Blood trickled down her slender, scarred neck, staining her collar. Ruby knew her own throat looked much the same. "You want to taste it."

"Fuck you."

"If you ask nicely," Anya murmured. She bent down, pressing her bloody lips against Ruby's. It couldn't be called a kiss—more a claim, a consumption, a communion—as Anya licked into Ruby's mouth. The ironic taste was unceasing, copper and sharp, tangy human flooding every bit of Ruby's senses, and when Anya pulled away, Ruby almost whimpered.

"Fuck you," Ruby croaked.

"You're not very convincing. You broke into my apartment and intended to use me as James Theaker used me—as a body, as a means to an end—but you don't even know the truth," Anya said and cupped her face with a bloody palm. "He killed nobody. The monster you seek is me, and I want more."

Ruby was trembling now, her fingers shaking with the urge to reach, and grab, and touch, and hurt, and kill, but

Anya's crimson smile—the first smile Ruby had ever seen the woman offer—stopped her in her tracks.

"What do you want from me?" Ruby asked.

Anya hummed and pressed her lips to the ruined skin beneath Ruby's chin. "I want to consume you. I want you to be reborn. I want to kill you, and I want to keep you." Anya's voice sent vibrations through her skin, down her spine. "I want you to choose, I think. Do you want to feel what Theaker—what I—did to those women, what his name will carry for the rest of my quiet life, or do you want to reach inside my body and pull me out by the fistful? Do you want to kill me, Ruby?"

The question hung in the air, all but rhetorical.

"I want," Ruby whispered, trailing off. Anya's pupils were blown. Flesh and gore reddened her lips. "I want…"

In one clean motion, Anya brought the blade to Ruby's wrist, severed the robe that held her to the bed, and placed the handle in Ruby's free hand. Ruby pressed the blade to Anya's throat, pushing until blood welled up and glided down the silver edge.

"I want to know how it feels to wield life and death," Ruby whispered.

Anya tucked a strand of loose hair behind Ruby's ear. "Let me show you how it feels, then. Let me recreate you the way you wanted Theaker to."

Ruby applied more pressure but Anya didn't flinch, even as she began to bleed in earnest. Instead, she pushed forward and kissed Ruby, leaned over her until blood fell onto Ruby's chest and jaw, mingling with Ruby's own lifeforce. Their bodies felt as if they were one. When Ruby pulled the weapon from

Anya's throat, Anya used it to cut Ruby's bonds. When Ruby threw the blade to the floor, it bounced off of a bookshelf and stained the carpet crimson.

When Anya kissed her, it was silent, and Ruby made her choice.

NEIGHBORLY

AQUINO LOAYZA

Thud. Thud. Craaasssh. BANG! With that, I put my spoon down and glared upward at my ceiling with contempt. I could deal with the apartment rattling when the train passed. I could plan for that. There was a schedule, a soothing rhythm in its inevitability. The noise emanating from above had no pattern. Anarchic like the cold, bustling city streets. What was the point of living between four walls if the chaos bled in?

I pushed myself out of the chair and looked at the television; the news was going on about urban blight. They found another person dead in their apartment. It was enough to make a man go mad. *BANG! Craaasssh! BANG!* I had enough of the noises from above.

Eyeing the door, I contemplated how to approach the situation. I had called the police previously, but with all the chaos, there was nothing they could do. Lies, of course. They could do something, anything, to stop the madness.

There was plenty to make good men turn bad these days, and sometimes I *really* wanted to go bad. What could stop me? The police? No, no, no, they were too busy with all the *chaos*.

I had decided what to do. I could talk to my neighbor. Everybody liked to speak. Every day someone tried talking to me, telling me things that must've been terribly important. I never listened. I couldn't. There was too much going on, all the noises, cars honking, people selling CDs, drugs, jewelry. It didn't matter what it was. They all wanted money. For what? To pay for walls that couldn't even stop *chaos* from bleeding in?

Blinking, I realized I had exited my apartment into the hallway. Lights flickered. The landlord never cared much to fix anything so long as the checks came in. The city used to be so beautiful. Apartments like these brought all walks of life into town. Now a hollowed-out skeleton, nothing left but vultures and those down on their luck, like me. Barely able to scrape by, with no opportunity to move on to something better, something brighter.

Then there was the malodorous *stench* descending from upstairs. The fragrance was followed by another crash and muffled yelling, as if on cue: "Enough is enough."

The voice was harsh, gravelly, and foreign. Yet, it was my own. It had been so long since anyone stopped yapping to listen. Nobody ever listened anymore. Always talking, either about themselves or the weather or the *chaos*. I could go on forever, but what would it do? I'm nothing but a cog. The machine keeps going, inevitable like the sunset or the train shaking my apartment. I'm sure it was pretty once, just like the city used to be.

Wasting no more time in my head, I walked to the stairway. The elevator was still broken. Occasionally there would be attempts to fix it, but it always reverted to its normal state of disrepair. The staircase served as the spine of a decaying warehouse-turned-dwelling. Humans latched on to each landing as though they were scavengers, and the last pieces of the carcass had yet to be consumed. As I made my way up to the next landing, I saw a man defecating in the corner.

"Toilet doesn't flush. It never does. Do you want to join me?" the man asked. He flicked his eyes over to me as he tilted his head.

"No, I don't have to go. I haven't eaten today. I never get to eat these days," I told him.

He nodded before going back to his task. I opened the door and made my way to the floor above.

Thud! Thud! Bang! Craaasssh! The muffled screams that followed echoed off the crudely painted walls. With each step, my dread rose, my feet rapidly approaching the apartment behind the auditory debauchery that hijacked my peaceful evening.

Would my neighbor listen? I knew I must do something, *anything*, to make the madness stop. There was so much of it these days. It even seeped into the four walls. What was the point of working if there was no peace?

My knuckles slammed on the metal door. Cold steel made a dull *thud*. Before the pain registered, the door opened as if someone had been waiting for me to show up. A pale man with shallow cheekbones stood in the doorframe, his eyes glowing yellow in the dark hallway. Behind him, screaming sounded.

"Can I help you? Do you want to come in?"

"No, I don't want to come in, but I will. You can help me," I said, stepping inside the apartment. The decrepit abode was dimly lit, the only light coming from an explicit film filling the television–a lustful display, men locked into action. The moaning explained the muffled screams.

"Do you want to watch it? I enjoy it. It helps me relax. You should relax, too."

"I don't want to watch it, but it's very nice. I'm sure you relax all the time. You have lovely cheekbones. I'm your neighbor. We share these four walls." I couldn't help but stare at his figure, a warm body like mine. It was amazing how gorgeous people could be.

"We aren't neighbors. I don't live here. I'm just here to relax. Did I mention that television is playing adult content? You should watch it, they don't make these anymore. You look like you need to relax, too." The film on the screen was undoubtedly adult, two men sharing a hedonistic embrace, filmed in an era when things had not been so terrible. Back when the world was a more decent place.

"Who are you if you're not my neighbor? You're too beautiful to be from the chaos. It's here with us, in these four walls. What's the point of working if it bleeds in?"

"Do you bleed?" he asked me, and I had to think about it. No, I couldn't remember a time I had bled. I only knew the color from the television. Sometimes I heard about people bleeding while I rode the train that shook the apartments, slow and soothing, predictable in its rhythm.

"I haven't bled before. Maybe I can. I don't know."

"Do you want to bleed? It's relaxing, like watching an adult movie. I helped your neighbor relax."

It hadn't registered as anything particularly strange. It wouldn't be very neighborly of me to ask what he meant. That was between the lovely man and my neighbor. How lucky my neighbor was, to have such a captivating man bleed into his walls! There was so much chaos out there. He was rather fortunate. All this man wanted to do was relax. Who could fault him?

"I don't know. Does it hurt? I don't like to hurt, but I do like your cheekbones. You're exquisite. Are you from this rancid city?" The city rarely birthed people like him anymore. Things weren't getting better. No matter how hard he tried, it just kept getting worse. Maybe relaxing wouldn't be so bad, maybe bleeding wouldn't be so bad.

"I have never bled. I help others bleed. I help others relax. That's what relaxes me."

That made all the sense in the world. I hadn't remembered why I'd come up here, just that his eyes had taken me in. Where was my neighbor? I am sure he didn't mind. It wasn't like I was the chaos. I didn't bleed in. I hadn't bled in my entire life. Plus, I didn't want to make a good man go bad.

"Where is my neighbor? I don't want to track gore all over his apartment. It's lovely, like your cheekbones. Beautiful, like a statue—this city used to have so many statues. Not anymore. They're gone." It was then that I caught another whiff of that distinct scent. It reminded me of urban sprawl rot, but there was something more organic about it. In a city where the arbor had long since died, all that remained living

were humans themselves, no birds or trees to speak of.

"I killed him. He was so worried about the things that make good men go bad. He couldn't relax. I tried so hard to make him relax. There's so much of it in this city, so much *chaos*. I come to their homes and try to help. But they just won't enjoy our time. *You* would enjoy our time."

He was the chaos bleeding into the four walls. It didn't make sense. The city was ugly, steel behemoths overlooking sludge-filled streams that were once rushing rivers. He was disarming, so calm, and his cadence had a rhythm to it, predictable despite his words being anything but. It was enough to make the alarms blaring in my head subside. I wanted to hear what he said next.

"I suppose I have to kill you too. Not that the cops will do anything. No, no, no, they are too busy. It's enough to make a good man go bad. Have you gone bad? Do you bleed? We'll find out."

I stayed in place. Morbid curiosity took hold of me, a primal sense—wanting to experience something, anything, different from the pervasive feeling of dissatisfaction.

"What if I don't want to bleed? What if I don't want to make a mess? Can I still relax? Can we relax together?" It was an innocuous enough question. Being a murderer didn't absolve other human desires, even if ritualistically. I rested my hand on his shoulder, trying to massage the tension out of him. His collarbone was exposed, perfect like the rest of him. A statue, even if he brought the *chaos* in.

He touched the base of my neck and stared into my eyes before planting his lips on mine. I felt a sharp object slice its

way into my stomach.

"You *do* bleed, see? Don't worry. I'm a janitor. I love to clean." He pulled away from me as he spoke. I felt no pain, but the growing pool of red on his other hand suggested his observation was accurate.

It was enough to make a good man go bad. The chaos had bled into all four walls, and I hadn't seen the point until now. It was enthralling, like him. He was so breathtaking I didn't care that I bled, only that I made a mess in the apartment. It wasn't very neighborly of me.

"I can clean it up," I said. "I promise."

"There's no need to clean. Just relax. I need to finish that movie, anyway." The statue turned his lips upward in a smile, genuine ecstasy on his face. Why was it so hard to relax before? The apartment shook as the train rattled by. There was a schedule, a rhythm I found soothing in its inevitability, not unlike the beating of my heart. *Thud. Thud.*

Thud. Thud, but this time it wasn't my heart. It was banging on the door before it flung open.

"FREEZE! PUT YOUR HANDS UP! WE ARE HERE TO DO SOMETHING, ANYTHING, TO STOP THIS MADNESS!"

The police pushed through with their rifles in hand, which resembled a custodian's broom, ready to tidy the unruly mess the *chaos* had made. Never mind, the beautiful demigod was a janitor. They didn't understand his genius or that he loved to clean. *Bang! Craaasssh.* I fell to the ground. Ichor poured out of me.

"No, no, no. Don't you have somewhere else to be? There's so much out there. It's enough to make good men go

bad." I nodded at the statue's words as I rested on the ground. He was right. There was so much evil out there. I wanted to go bad, but I wanted to relax even more.

What was the point of the four walls? What was the point of working? Grinding until my hands were riddled with calluses? To come home and sleep between those four walls, wondering what would bleed in? It was not a very good life to lead. Not now, the city had become a cesspool, where arbors and avian beasts went to extinguish their flickering flames of vitality.

"PUT YOUR HANDS UP, OR WE WILL SHOOT! DO YOU BLEED?" an officer asked.

The room spun. I could hear the beautiful statue make his way toward their voices, shuffling his feet, weaponless. The glint of his silvery blade jutted from my side. Blackness enveloped my sight as the sound of bullets smacked against stone. A dull *thud* followed suit as the gunfire stopped.

"Call an ambulance. He's going to be okay! It's going to be okay!" The voice sounded distant. I did not know if I would be okay. I did not know if I *could* be okay. The last beautiful thing in this city has died, and I would soon join him.

As the sounds of life dulled and the world blackened, I shuttered my eyes. When I opened them again, I found myself in a beautiful garden full of birds and trees with no walls for *anything* to bleed in. A finely carved marble statue stood central in the courtyard, his mindless gaze piercing me with an intensity beyond words. Yet I knew what he wanted me to do, what he wanted me to feel.

So I finally, truly, relaxed. The chaos be damned.

THE SILENCE OF BROKEN THINGS

XAN VAN ROOYEN

Albums: THE SILENCE OF BROKEN THINGS
EmEff
2023

GENRE: alt metal / dark electronica
LABEL: independent
REVIEWED: April 25, 2023

If rage-filled revenants made music, it might sound like this: moments of eerie tenderness juxtaposed with screeching guitars and preternatural vocals that could be wailing a grocery list and would still be transcendent.

Like a scalpel to the brain, the mysterious internet sensation known only as EmEff delivers an EP weaving meaningful moments of stillness through an otherwise frenetic sonic landscape that defies categorization but leans heavily toward dark electronica with industrial metal undercurrents and haunting vocals. The four track offering will leave you gasping for breath and desperate to know more about this artist who has captivated online imagination.

Track One: They Who Have Escaped the Weight of Darkness *— buoyed by djenting guitars and strung-out 808s, the opening track is an ode to nightmare with strangled screaming filtered over a deluge of synthesized melodies all vying for harmonic control. The unusual chord progressions and pained voice certainly lend this piece an otherworldly quality as if something beyond the veil were tearing its way through the frequencies.*

The silence is a pall poured over the cluttered shelves, clotted thick between the abandoned and forgotten components: speakers ripped from their housings, mixing-board entrails spilled across moldy floorboards, an old Korg leaning lopsided in a corner—innards sparking with bad connections as it twitches against inevitable death.

Memories hover and flit in the stillness, shedding the dust of recollection like moth wings; memories of serving on stage to gods of metal, of thrumming fresh tracks in studios crackling with potential, of fingers coaxing twelve-bar Blues from spotless keys.

There are ghosts too—and worse—tangled in the shadows, cobwebbed across the eviscerated electronics and forlorn instruments cowering beneath the weight of being labeled obsolete.

For Emery, the second-hand store—called Sonicks (but the incorrect spelling irritates Emery so much they refuse to acknowledge the name altogether)—tucked down a nameless side street is a veritable cornucopia. The shop survived thanks only to the resurgence of interest in vinyls, stacked in bins sorted by genre for the mostly twenty-somethings carrying eco-cups of fairtrade coffee in thrift-store tweed. Emery had once been chased out by the girl who worked weekends and clearly had no understanding of sub-genre, for re-homing several vinyls erroneously filed under 'hard rock', in the 'alternative rock' bin.

Despite that unpleasantness, Emery still comes once a week to trawl through the detritus of the music industry. Just when they thought they'd scoured every inch of the sepulchral back room, they'd unearth a hidden box and hold their breath as they peeled open decades' old cardboard in the hopes of finding treasure.

It was usually trash: components long past the point of salvaging, bits and bobs from another era that Emery's engineering skills, forged in middle school shop class and online tutorials, had no way of resurrecting for modern use.

They'd scored an old laptop from a friend of a friend and had jury-rigged scavenged hardware to create a functional, if unreliable, DAW for their composition purposes. Maybe if they'd managed to keep a job long enough to actually save some cash, they'd be able to afford a semi-decent system that didn't run on muttered curses and Emery's indefatigable stubbornness.

But Emery didn't know how to keep their thoughts to

themselves, not in the fast food franchise where they'd been hired to bus tables and not express opinion on the nutritional value of the menu, not at the movie theater where they'd been paid to fill boxes of popcorn and not maintain a running commentary on all the problematic actors, encouraging would-be moviegoers to boycott certain films, and certainly not when they'd been employed—for all of five hours—at a generic clothing store where they'd been compelled to inform shoppers of the conditions in the sweat shops fabricating the ersatz high fashion items.

Self-righteous. Pretentious. Sanctimonious. Asshole.

Emery had been slapped with all of those, which were still better than the names they'd been called on the kindergarten playground (like the one that rhymed with discard). Those names were later punctuated with fists until Emery had come to realize the mediocre education they were receiving at the hands of over-worked, under-paid, not-even-remotely motivated and truly-exasperated teachers wasn't going to get them anywhere in life they couldn't take themself, and without the tie-dye blossoming of bruises across their skin. If Dad had been around, maybe they would've persisted until graduation and managed to preserve what little self-esteem hadn't already been eroded to dust…

Dust. Emery sneezes into the crook of their elbow, the sound violent as it shatters the stillness. They apologize under their breath, not noticing the way a particularly oleaginous shadow shivers in response.

Turning their attention back to scavenging, Emery continues to explore the tomb with reverent fingers, long and

stained black by blown out self-poked tattoos. Only Emery can tell the *coda* from the treble clef, the *del segno* from the *mf* pricked into the skin they wash at least thirty times a day.

Despite having caught the sneeze with their elbow, Emery feels the itch at the base of their thumb, the need to wash their hands—for the requisite twenty seconds with a good deal of soap—smoldering like lit kindling at the back of their mind. It will have to wait though, music has always been more important. More than clean hands, more than soft clothes without razor-blade seams or cheese-grater labels, more than nutritionally balanced meals—not so easy to come by on what little money trickles into their account as strangers around the world stream their music—more than black coffee (no milk or sugar ever), more than water (never fizzy) or even air, Emery needs music.

If Emery could survive on rhythm and melody alone, they would. In fact, they did for the majority of the past year before one of their songs went viral. Emery dislikes this analogy, as if their music were *infecting* people and making them sick instead of providing a panacea. Still, that unexpected propagation netted them a small but dedicated following whose generosity clad their bones in flesh again and allowed them to move from a dumpster-scavenged tent in the park into the seedy studio apartment they share with at least three mice. Technically they should've been living with their aunt who'd inherited them when Dad died, but she'd seemed about as keen on that as Emery: both preferred pretending the other didn't exist. Even so, money appeared in Emery's account every month until they'd turned eighteen last summer, which was when they'd relocated to the park.

The clouds must've thinned outside allowing a single beam of light to pierce the gloom through the tiny grime-smeared window. Emery's brain rejects what their senses have communicated, rejects the notion that the shadows moved when their own shadow remains firmly fixed in place—as it should be—sprawling behind them. Emery's brain rejects the sudden chill carding through the fine hairs on the back of their neck or the dribble of icy sweat escaping their left armpit. They rub at the spot with annoyance, determined to ignore the roil in their belly telling them they're not alone, to turn around, to run a risk assessment. This is their sanctuary, here where they are alone in the silence—even though it makes Emery's heart ache to hear such absence amid items made for sound—perfectly alone in the dim lighting that doesn't strain their eyes, in the pleasantly musty soup due to lack of ventilation without the threat of sudden assault by someone overzealous in the application of deodorant.

Following the beam of light, fingers dancing paradiddles across the now visible motes, Emery carefully pushes aside a box of cables revealing a smaller box not yet caked in the dirt of neglect.

Emery's heart contracts. This is new. It wasn't here last week. The cardboard—scuffed and torn in one corner—is otherwise pristine. No logo, not a single defining feature. With trembling fingers, Emery extracts the box from its haphazard burial, apologizing again when their elbow knocks the decapitated body of an Ibanez. A flicker of shadow creeps closer. Emery blinks, but the darkness persists, a cool press

like a gentle hand against their back.

Inside the box sits a set of headphones, folded up in the fetal possession, curled like a sleeping flower, waiting for someone to unfurl the ear pieces. Emery inspects their find. Knock-offs probably, judging by the lack of branding. The earpieces aren't even marked left or right, the head band is hard plastic without any cushioning—an easy fix—and there's no port for a jack. Bluetooth then—not ideal, but workable.

A murmur, like the whisper of wind through summer thick grass.

Emery raises the headphones to their ears. Ah, a crackle of static perhaps caused by a loose connection. Now they know why the headphones were so unceremoniously tossed, but the longer Emery listens, the more certain they become: there's a pattern to the scratch and click, a rhythm desperate for release, a melody trapped in a web of frequencies. Perhaps the headphones are still paired with a distant device, holding on to whatever slivers of sound are being conveyed along ultra-high radio waves.

Emery re-ensconces the headphones in their dowdy box and uncrumples their limbs from the disorderly pile they'd fallen into when their focus had been on their find and not their surroundings. With more proprioceptive awareness, Emery leaves the back room, choosing to ignore—because it's impossible—how their washed-out, threadbare sweatshirt not only seems at least three shades blacker than it was when they put it on this morning, but is also heavier as if they've been caught in the rain. The shirt is dry though, and Emery knows this because wet fabric against their skin feels the way

Emery imagines being flayed alive must feel: like putting on woolen gloves.

Emery slides a pristine note on the cashier's desk and waggles the box, gesticulating with it toward the back room marked 'Junk' where everything is priced for donation at the customer's discretion. They once commented about that—and the unfair label of *junk*—to the shop owner who threatened to ban them from the store altogether, so now Emery keeps their lips clamped firmly between their incisors to prevent accidental opinions leaking from their tongue.

Payment accepted, Emery takes a bracing breath and exits the store. It's five-hundred and thirty-two steps from Sonicks—the errant k really makes their skin prickle almost as badly as the thought of touching wet soil, almost as much as the unusually heavy sweatshirt dragging at the sharp points where clavicle meets shoulder—to their studio. They've done this dozens of times, they can do it again. Cradling the box and repeating "It's not junk, it's not junk" under their breath, Emery begins the hurried trek home with wisps of shadow peeling from their shirt.

Track Two: The Scar Tissue Map of Home – perhaps the most dramatic track, with a grating industrial beat driving it relentlessly toward the climax, this piece is a meander through aggressive dissonance desecrating the ear with myriad modulations in clashing minor keys. Halfway through this 13 minute threnody, the music builds in a tornado of wailing strings before shattering into a sparse and subdued piano part. The ending is a minimalist oscillation between sound

and silence threading repetitive melodies with the murmured echoing lyric "the lemniscate of memory severed".

Shoes neatly planted at the door, Emery sucks in several mouthfuls of cool air. The apartment is cold—not much point paying for heating when they detest sweating and have never really felt the need for jackets. Not even in the depths of winter with six inches of snow on the ground. It was another reason they were teased at school. Dad wanted them to wear a snowsuit like the other kids, wanted them to don mittens and a hat; every winter became a war.

When Emery had tried to explain how the wool made their head feel like it was on fire despite the protection of their thick curls, or how they'd rather stick their hands into boiling water than put their fingers into gloves, Dad would wear an expression Emery later came to understand as disbelief, then pity. Dad had tried to understand Emery's autism—neurons firing in atypical patterns, senses overloaded, synapses lacking pruning—but even Dad had mistaken explanations for excuses and didn't always have the patience for Emery unmasked.

Now, Emery shucks the too-heavy sweatshirt, leaving it coiled in a sinuous heap in the middle of the living room which is sometimes where they sleep, but mostly where they make music. Another thing Dad didn't like was the fact Emery hardly slept, and definitely wouldn't at a time convenient for their dad who'd worked two jobs to keep a roof over their heads and microwaveable meals in the freezer.

The apartment is dark, kept in a permanent state of gray ambiance to suit Emery's crepuscular preferences. They fire

up the laptop, concerned by the labored whirring of the fans. It sounds a lot like Dad did toward the end, when his tumor-riddled lungs had wheezed their last.

Disconnecting their current headphones—semi-decent studio ones someone gifted them off their wishlist last year when they'd had their moment of fame—Emery removes the new headphones from the box and a notification pops up on the screen informing them the new device is already paired.

Skeptical, and somewhat disconcerted by the fact a stain is spreading across the carpet from the shriveled pile of sweatshirt, Emery tentatively pulls the headphones over their ears, tucking away unruly curls and making sure the foam doesn't pinch piercings or cartilage.

The static hums with an ebbing tide intensity.

Emery went to the beach once, screamed when their bare feet hit the sand, and kept screaming until Dad bundled them back into the car, chain-smoking out the window with one hand while gently stroking Emery's shoulder with the other. They noticed the gulls then, the wind, the crash and suck of the waves against the beach. They listened, soaking in the sound, eyes closed and ears open, as their frantic heartbeat attuned to the roar and recession of the churning water.

They feel it now, the desire to drown in the sound decanting from the headphones into their ears, a pair of digital seashells. And beneath the layers of static, stitched into the texture of the suppressed rhythm and yearning melody, a voice—as gritty as the sand, as sticky as the salt air, whispering, calling, demanding…

Emery opens their DAW and starts a new project. The

old Yamaha keyboard flashes assurance of connection and Emery rests their fingers against the pleasing pattern of white and black mimicked in their skin. Their arms are mottled with homemade tattoos, snatches of Dad's favorite songs, lyrics they never wanted to forget, interesting chord progressions, moments etched into flesh to be recalled even when their brain decides to forget. They stare—bewildered and bemused with panic plucking at their senses like fingers testing newly fitted guitar strings—as black smudges spread down their arms, the ink swimming beneath their skin. It pools in Emery's finger tips, making them twitch and dance against a sudden biting cold, striking the keys with fervent velocity.

Track Three: Adumbral Adoration, or, the War Waged Between our Lungs – the first five minutes are a slow contemplation of melancholy punctuated by hectic drums making good on the second half of a title that has spawned numerous fan theories. The lyrics, posted by the artist themself in a barely legible scrawl, hint at a soul unable to reconcile seemingly disparate emotions (dig dreams from my eyes, suck fever from my veins, don't give in—just give in to this misfire brain, all shadow-catcher gray matter). This becomes even more apparent in the second half of the over-wrought track where moments of silence give way to virtuosic guitar motifs that'll leave the listener feeling gently caressed one moment and sucker punched the next.

For weeks, Emery subsists on frequencies and roiling emotion they cannot name. They feel themselves unraveling,

the tight stitches holding them together ripped apart as they bleed across the keys, blood and shadow spawning note after flickering note on their monitor.

For weeks, they lay tracks upon tracks, sculpting delicate harmony and intricate rhythms, mixing and mastering in sonic lapidary until every facet of the music is honed perfection.

They scratch absentmindedly at the scabs caught like beetles in their tangled curls from where the headphone band has cut a rill across their scalp. Red stripes their neck in vertical staves and Emery rubs stained fingers over the dried stickiness. The album is complete—EP really, only a handful of tracks clocking in at 41 minutes and fifty-two seconds. But it's done and there's no need for prolixity.

The whispers in Emery's ears are less urgent now, no longer a pick-ax hammering at their brain but a soothing susurrus as the smudges winnowing beneath their skin retreat along sinews, withdrawing their dark tendrils from fingers and arms to curl a single frond around each ear.

Emery grinds their teeth against the excruciating exit that leaves them with a hollow absence in their bones, their shrinking veins crying out in want of phantom pressure.

Don't go, don't leave me, not again, please stay, please, please the words scrape from swollen tongue and blistered lips, the cauterized wound behind Emery's ribs rupturing anew.

Grief had been explained by the dictionary in neat little letters, by videos online in cute cartoons or by sad-faced psychologists with visual aids, by real people reeling through anger, by those still bargaining or in denial. Emery mapped

out the five stages and waited patiently for their own journey to commence. It never did. For Emery, and for Dad, death was a relief: an end to stertorous breathing, to pain, and waiting for the inexorable.

Perhaps they accidentally skipped straight to acceptance without realizing. They miss Dad—his laughter and the way he made the perfect cup of coffee, the way he always removed the labels from Emery's clothes by unpicking the stitching and not just cutting them out which still left sharp edges. Emery misses Saturday walks in the park and the way Dad always knew exactly when to hand over the Ear Defenders, knew without asking what Emery wanted on their hot dog from the food truck parked on the corner because it was always the same; misses Dad's protein oatmeal on Sunday mornings with the cupful of berries for fiber on the side and their favorite spoon set on the left of the bowl, but most of all, Emery misses their Sunday evening jam sessions: Dad on his old Strat, Emery alternating between the faulty keyboard with a bunch of missing keys in the upper octave or the steel-string they'd rescued on their first visit to Sonicks together. Dad laughed when Emery grumbled about the k and, although that made Emery feel bad at the time, they miss Dad's laughter too, miss Dad's smile even though his teeth were crooked and wore nicotine stains, miss the crunchy lines around his mouth, and his big hand engulfing Emery's smaller one, the contact bearable and oddly reassuring.

Emery makes a fist, nails grown long cutting crescents into their palm as heat builds behind their eyes and their nose starts to run.

Dad didn't want to be buried. He made Emery promise there'd be no funeral, no prayers, no eulogy. Just flames and ash, and a nondescript urn, the contents of which Emery mixed with tattoo ink and laid beneath their skin in shaky lines with a sewing needle at first, then later with a coil machine fashioned from salvaged parts.

Emery rubs their arms—thinner now, veins and tendons straining like cables against desiccated skin—tracing the words and symbols, a litany of memory. The voice in the headphones is no longer a garbled static but words Emery can parse in a voice they know, an echo from the time before death became a reality instead of a distant inevitability. They tighten the band of the headphones, not caring about the cracked scabs and warmth trickling down their neck, press the headphones hard against their ears savoring the roar and murmur, the fading laughter, the final words spluttered between bubbling breaths—Dad's lungs already hemorrhaging—and Emery not knowing how it would all be okay no matter how many times Dad said it.

On the couch that is sometimes a bed, although they can't remember when last they slept, Emery tucks their knees to their chest, elbows folded over legs and hands still clamped over the headphones as the death-bed mantra plays on a fading loop. Tears burn acid trails across their cheeks, a wetness they cannot stand, but this time they don't care as their body vibrates in time with the music flooding their ears, their music, the tracks playing in sequence—the four stages of Emery's grief.

As the final notes fade, Emery releases their hold on the

headphones to hug themself instead, eyes closed, breathing slowing as sleep closes a fist around their brain, as the headphones slip from their curls—spent and empty—as the shadows drip oily from their ears and rise in smoky streamers from the tattoos on their arms. Only ink and memory now, no longer ghost-tainted. Emery exhales a steady breath, blowing apart the diaphanous remains of shadow, releasing them both.

__Track Four: Remember Me in Cadential Six-Fours__ — the final track brings to a close an impressive 42-minute emotional roller-coaster that will feel too short for some, and too long by half for others. The journey comes full circle as we return once more to the EP's opening guitar riffs underscored by bass as heavy as a black hole's gravity, punctuated by unexpected moments of silence. Wrangled into an abbreviated sonata form that skips the traditional recapitulation, Remember Me staggers from the Development straight into a coda, which shifts through the titular chords as the track eventually lets out the breath it was very aware it was holding.

To listen to this album is to witness a wound bleeding, scabbing, and starting to heal. Whether the wound is self-inflicted and kept raw by navel-gazing, or the result of a vulnerable soul injured by a harsh world remains unknown as EmEff stays firmly cocooned in enigma even as their music sends out radioactive ripples across the indie scene. Love it or hate it, The Silence of Broken Things will certainly leave you feeling bruised and grateful for the ache.

DIFFERENT

ASHLEY LEZAK

"Mommy?" Abigail croaked. She fought to stay awake. Something beeped rhythmically off to her right.

"I'm here, sweetheart," her mother said from the left.

She held Abigail's hand and stroked it in the same spot, over and over. Abigail tried to snatch it away on instinct, but her limb didn't respond. Once she'd taken a moment to breathe, the repetition felt soothing, so she relaxed and let her mother keep going.

She managed to unstick her eyelids, squinting at the brightness. Her head felt like it was full of cotton but she was able to turn just enough to find her mother's face. Her mother's eyes were blue with a little ring of gray around the edge of her iris. Abigail had never noticed that before. She returned her mother's tentative smile.

Her mother pulled her hands back to cover her face.

Her father squeezed his eyes shut. "It's okay, honey. Me

too," he said, voice cracking.

Abigail managed to shift her head a little more.

"What happened, Dad?"

Her father's eyelashes were wet and clumped. They were thicker than her mother's, another thing she'd never noticed before. He opened his mouth like he wanted to say something, but it just drifted closed again.

"It's okay, sweetheart. You're better now," her mother said between heaving sobs.

Something must have happened. Abigail closed her eyes and took a deep breath, like her mother and Miss Julie taught her to. She checked in with her body, but it felt fine. There was just that fuzzy feeling in her head, like she'd slept way too long or not at all.

A woman she didn't recognize moved closer and said, "Can I check your eyes? It'll only take a minute, I promise." Before she finished speaking, white light seared Abigail's vision. She made a noise, trying to slap the light away. Her right hand got stuck; something tugged at her finger. Her left hand came up, but only with a lot of effort, like it was asleep.

"Stop! I don't like that," she cried out. "Mama, make it stop!"

"It's okay Abigail, Dr. Ramirez just wants to make sure you're okay. You've been asleep for a long time," her mother said, catching Abigail's free hand mid-swat. Her hold was firm, but not hard enough to hurt. One of them was shaking, just a little.

When the light faded, Abigail cracked open one eye, just to be sure it was safe. It was hard to see past the spots, but

she looked at her mother, then to her father, who had moved himself out of the way. They both nodded, so Abigail nodded too.

"Thank you, Abby," the doctor started.

Abigail's father lurched a bit and opened his mouth again, catching Dr. Ramirez's attention, but her mother grabbed his hand and shook her head. A feeling nagged at the back of Abigail's mind.

Dr. Ramirez glanced at Abigail's parents before continuing, "I need you to look straight ahead, hard as you can. It'll be really bright, but if you're very good I'll give you candy. How does that sound?"

"I like the green ones, they make my mouth pucker," Abigail said automatically, like it was practiced.

Dr. Ramirez winked at her. "Then I'll make sure it's a green one."

Dr. Ramirez turned off her light when she was done and smiled again, offering a green candy from a pocket in her white coat. Abigail smiled back, blinking away teary spots. She reached for the candy and was happy to find that her arms were working a little better now. Her mouth watered, anticipating the onslaught of sour.

She must have been making a face, because her father inhaled sharply and her mother asked, "What's the matter, Abigail?"

Abigail pushed the candy into her cheek and said, "I don't like it."

"But green has *always* been your favorite," her father said.

Her mother pinched her father's arm but kept her eyes on Abigail. *Why isn't he allowed to say that?*

"Do you need to spit it out?" her mother asked.

Abigail considered for a moment, rolling the candy around in her mouth.

"No, it's not that bad. I'll just finish it." Her head felt light enough to shake by this point, but something tugged against her scalp, stopping her.

"Tastes often change after the procedure," Dr. Ramirez said.

Her mother cleared her throat.Abigail reached toward her scalp. It was gooey, with wires coming out of each gob, but her hair was exactly where it belonged. She let out a breath. Dr. Ramirez handed Abigail a tissue to wipe off her fingers, watching her closely.

"I promise we'll take those off soon. In the meantime, if you'd like to sit up, you can use this," Dr. Ramirez said, pressing a remote into Abigail's hand.

She had to lift the remote to find the right button. The bed bent into a sitting position, whining loudly the whole way.

Everyone's eyes were glued to her as the bed did its business. Abigail's mother stood. Her face was still splotchy, but the tears were all done.

"We'll be just out in the hall if you need us, sweetheart," she said.

Abigail nodded the best she could. Her mother tugged her father to follow as Dr. Ramirez led them out.

Abigail tuned out the screeching bed and waited for it to reach a comfortable angle.

Her father pushed her into the parking lot. She could walk just fine, but Dr. Ramirez had said the wheelchair was "non-negotiable."

Her mother walked ahead and opened the back door for Abigail, who wrinkled her nose and prepared for the bad car smell. When she was little, she used to hold her breath so hard she'd pass out, but when she was about eight, she'd finally learned to breathe through her mouth.

Her father rolled her next to the open door and she still hadn't noticed the smell. She took a closer look, just to be sure it was the same car. Her father locked the wheelchair and offered her his arm, but she hesitated.

"Dad, did you get a new car?"

Her father straightened and looked the car over, frowning. "What? No. Why would you think that?"

"It smells different."

Her father leaned into the car and took an audible whiff.

"Smells the same to me, honey," he said.

Her mother shut the trunk and came around the passenger's side, wiping dust from her pants as she always did. She looked between Abigail and her father. "What's going on? Why aren't you in the car yet?"

Her father shrugged. "Apparently, the car smells different."

Her mother's eyes narrowed a bit. "That's nonsense."

"But—" Abigail started, but her mother gave her *that* look, and she stopped.

As Abigail climbed into her booster seat, she checked the

floor between the back footwells. The years-old stain from when the drive-thru changed their orange juice supplier was still there. She'd taken a big gulp on a hot day and immediately spat it all over the floor. It had taken months for the smell of rotting orange juice to dissipate to tolerable levels.

While her mother buckled her in, Abigail wondered if something had happened to her nose. Her mother answered all her questions with tearful orders to not worry. Her father had told her that the doctors made it all better, but he couldn't meet her eyes; she didn't ask him again. Abigail didn't remember being sick, but her memories were fuzzy and she had to chase down every thought.

The sun beamed through the tinted window, more heat than light. The wires between the telephone poles rose and fell like calm waves lapping the shore of the lake they visited every summer. Abigail counted them until she drifted off.

Her mother turned around in her seat. Only her nose was in focus; the rest of her face was blurry, like a watercolor painting ruined by a tipped rinsing cup. Her mouth opened, too big and so, so dark. She screamed at Abigail—horrible things: that she's a bad kid, that she's too difficult to love, that they wished they could take her back and get a good kid, a better kid.

Abigail choked on the smell of rotten orange juice. She tried to beg her father to make it stop but she couldn't speak, everything came out as horrible shrieks. Wet tears ran down her cheeks, making stray hairs stick to her face as she flailed. Her father turned and lunged for her. The car veered wildly

across the road, sending her flying in one direction as her father gripped her arm and yanked her in the other.

She suddenly found herself staring at the spotted flat ceiling of Miss Julie's office. Her mother was smashing her hands to make them fit into the arms of another child's empty skin. Miss Julie was stuffing her into the squelching steaming mess bit by bit, breaking bones and tearing flesh. Folding and crushing and stretching her until she was contained. She tried to fight but they were so much stronger and her new skin suit scratched and pulled and pinched, restricting her to the movements they wanted her to make. She screamed as one of them shoved candy down her throat and the other told her she was a *good girl*.

Abigail was startled awake as the car door opened. The seatbelt caught her jerking body. She still heard screaming. Someone unhooked the seatbelt and pulled her to the ground, hugging her tightly. She knew that body. The screaming stopped. She swallowed shards of glass. Her mother hummed as she rocked them both.

Abigail took a shallow ragged breath and tried to push out of the crushing embrace, but her mother only clutched harder.

Abigail finally got a grasp on her words and choked out, "Can't—breathe."

Her mother instantly released her. Abigail jolted forward and scrambled toward the awful little bushes next to the driveway. They weren't bothering her. They still smelled like her father after one of his long walks.

"Sweetheart, are you okay?"

"The bushes—I," Abigail started, but when she turned to face her mother she found concern. "I'm sorry, Mama, I had a bad dream and I got confused. I didn't mean to fight you."

She crawled back over and reached out. Her mother pulled Abigail into her lap and wrapped her in a tight embrace. She felt her mother's breath catch.

"Deep breaths, Mama. It's okay," Abigail said into her shoulder.

"Oh, honey," she said, choking back tears, helping Abigail to her feet. "I know. Everything's going to be okay. You go on in, I'll be right there."

As Abigail approached the front door, she realized the smell from the bushes didn't make it to the house, like she always thought it had.

She stepped inside and nearly tripped over a stuffed moose. She grinned and made a mad dash straight through the house. Moomoo was waiting for her at the back door. She dropped to her knees and waited, but the dog hesitated, letting out a low growl and a whimper.

"What's the matter, girl?" Abigail said, extending a hand for Moomoo to sniff.

Moomoo jumped at the sound of Abigail's voice. The dog leaned in for a sniff, cocking her head, whining. Abigail wiggled her fingers and frowned as Moomoo backed away. Then she circled Abigail, sniffing every inch she could reach, before sitting down and whimpering again.

Abigail grabbed a squeaky toy and sat on the deck, like her father had taught her when they first got Moomoo. She

offered the toy, giving it a squeaky squeeze. Moomoo shook out her fur and took a few steps, tail wagging tightly, nervously. Abigail moved too quickly. Moomoo retreated again. *Weird. Moomoo isn't a scared kind of dog.*

She sighed and laid back on the deck, stretching her arms above her head and watching wispy clouds float by, keeping Moomoo just inside her periphery.

After a few minutes of stalemate, Abigail got bored and sat up. Moomoo stiffened but decided to sniff Abigail again before finally pressing her head into her hand. Abigail delivered rigorous scratchies, earning a lick on the nose in return.

"Do I smell like medicine? Is that it? I was in the hospital, but I'm still me, promise!"

Moomoo tensed at her voice, but only for a moment. Abigail lifted the toy and threw it into the yard before making her way to the edge of the deck. She dangled her legs between the railings.

She rocked, looking between posts, but that didn't feel right, so she sat cross-legged on the picnic table. Moomoo joined her, pressing her hip against Abigail's.

A breeze rustled the trees, cool enough to give Abigail goosebumps. She watched Moomoo's nose wiggle. The neighbor's sprinklers were on. Everything felt dull and faded, like something was missing. Tears welled and she bit her lip to hold them back, wiping her eyes with her sleeve.

She and Moomoo both sighed as they got up. She gave Moomoo a few distracted pets. Maybe she was just hungry.

"I didn't expect *this*, though," Abigail's father said.

"Well, you're the one who pushed for it. I don't know what to tell you," Abigail's mother responded. Her parents were at the kitchen table and hadn't noticed her yet. "They did say there would be an adjustment period with—"

Her eyes darted to Abigail. Both parents tensed, just like the deer Abigail liked to watch at the edge of the woods behind their house. *There's a clear memory, finally.* Sitting in a tree in the yard, holding so still that a whole herd had grazed up to the trunk. Then they'd stiffened, first one, then the others; nostrils flaring, ears twitching, before disappearing into the woods.

Her mother shot up from the table with a smile stretched too tight. "Hi honey, did you need something?"

Abigail's stomach grumbled. "I think I'm hungry. Can I have a snack?"

"I actually have a sandwich right here for you, already made! Why don't you sit?"

Abigail nodded. Her mother sat her down in front of a plated sandwich and a glass of water. The water was cool and refreshing. She watched Moomoo chase a squirrel across the deck through the sliding door. She took a distracted bite of the sandwich and was met with strong flavors that somehow went well together. It wasn't her usual sandwich, but Abigail inhaled it, crust and all.

Her parents both stared at her. Her mother was sniffling again. Her father's face was blank, but his eyes were hard. Abigail usually had an easier time reading her father than her mother, but she had been struggling since the hospital. She was pretty sure this look was wary.

As she put a name to it, an image of a flashcard with a matching face popped into her head. She remembered it from Miss Julie's office.

Abigail brought her dishes to the sink to rinse. As she watched the water swirl around in the cup, she realized it wasn't hers. She turned it over in her hand: it was plastic, a little rough to the touch, not smooth like her mug. Her whole body stiffened, and something welled inside her. Her heart pounded in her ears.

She also hadn't been at her spot at the table, and the sandwich had been her father's sandwich. Tongue and mustard with chopped liver, not turkey, tomato, and Swiss. But she'd *liked* it? Her stomach churned, and the hairs on her neck stood up. Abigail gripped the counter and took a few shallow breaths, trying to calm down.

In, out. In. Out.

In.

Out.

As her breathing lengthened, her body unclenched. When she turned around, her mother had left the kitchen. She could hear her crying in the other room. Her father was still watching her.

"Everything okay?" he asked.

Abigail took a few more deep breaths. The feeling ebbed, leaving emptiness in its wake. "I—I was drinking out of the wrong cup."

"Oh, uh."

"There is no such thing as a wrong cup, sweetheart," her

mother said. She stood in the doorway, giving her father *that* look. Abigail hadn't heard her stop crying. Her father raised his hands, like he did when he was done playing with Moomoo, and retreated to the living room. Abigail heard him groan as he settled onto the couch.

Her mother was still looking at her, waiting for an answer. "Oh, of course. Sorry, Mama."

"That's okay sweetheart. Did you like your sandwich?"

"It wasn't my usual, but it was pretty good."

A smile bloomed across her mother's face, so bright and relieved that Abigail couldn't help but smile back.

"That's wonderful," her mother said, and then a touch of worry crept into her eyes. Her smile faltered. "I thought I might make something new for dinner tonight, how does that sound?"

Abigail took a moment to think. How *did* that sound? Her body was still working through the panic that had gripped her at the sink. The idea of a new dinner didn't absolutely repulse her, so she shrugged.

Her mother's smile returned. She wrapped Abigail in a quick hug, gently squeezing her upper arms as she whirled off to the fridge. "I'm sure you'll love it! Oh, I almost forgot, I also have a big kid toothpaste for you to try tonight."

Abigail wandered into the living room, trying to get some of the residual nervous energy out of her body. The mention of toothpaste had made her tense up again, but she didn't know why it would be upsetting. She hesitated before crossing in front of the TV.

"Hey Dad, I'm going up to my room, okay? I want..." She

trailed off. She used to go straight to her room after her snack, but couldn't remember why. She shook her head, trying to clear it. "Actually, can we maybe watch TV together or something?"

Her father fixed that unnerving stare on her again. "Oh, uh. Are you sure? You've been gone for a bit, I bet the dust would really catch the light just right today," he said.

"I just want to hang out and watch something together, I think. Is that okay?"

"Of course, did you want to watch your show? I can grab the computer and hook it up." He was fidgeting with his hands, tapping his fingers to his thumbs in a pattern. He noticed Abigail watching him and squeezed his hands together before placing them flat on his knees. His fingers sat there, still as the arms of a chair.

"I actually don't know, maybe just whatever you have on?"

Her father stared at her—*guarded*, that's what this look was. Abigail made her way to the couch and flopped into the corner piece next to him. He stiffened as she reached over to grab his arm but relaxed when she pulled it around her shoulders and snuggled into his side.

He was watching a nature documentary; it was fine. Not what she usually watched, but fine. Her mother joined them after a while, sitting on Abigail's other side. She squeezed Abigail's ankle and scooted in close. It felt right, being pressed between her parents, maybe she *was* just hungry earlier when everything felt wrong.

Her room was musty and dark. She wasn't sure just how long she'd been gone, but they must have left at night or first thing in the morning because Abigail *always* opened her curtains right after waking up.

The last of the afternoon sun streamed in and a blast of cool air hit her face. She closed her eyes and breathed deeply. When she turned around, she noticed dust flecks dancing in the sunbeams like glitter. It was pretty.

She turned, trying to reacquaint herself with the space. A glint caught her eye. She froze and adjusted her head until she caught it again. It was coming from a gap in the baseboard by her desk. She started toward it but stopped when she heard her mother humming down the hallway near her office.

Abigail snuck to her door and popped her head into the hall. She held her breath so she could focus better, but It didn't help. She tried a few more times but all it did was make her lightheaded. She held onto the door frame until she felt okay again and listened.

She could hear her father playing with Moomoo downstairs. Her mother was typing away. The clacking of her mechanical keyboard usually felt like being pecked by ducks, but Abigail had no issues tuning it out this time.

She turned the knob and walked the door closed before slowly releasing it. Once she was satisfied she wouldn't be interrupted, Abigail went about prying the lopsided section of baseboard off the wall. Behind it sat an old silver pencil box. She didn't remember putting it there.

It held a couple of pretty rocks, leaves, and a folded pamphlet. She accidentally crumbled a leaf while pulling the

pamphlet out, but she couldn't remember what could possibly be important enough about any of it to hide in the wall in the first place.

The pamphlet had clearly been ripped apart and taped back together with some big pieces missing. She struggled to smooth it out.

"Tragedy of autism" and "Successors have been shown to" and "Get back the child that" were overlaid on a silhouette of a family holding hands in front of a sunset. The other side had a website and part of a phone number.

Oh.

Oh.

Abigail sat quietly for a few minutes, staring at nothing, until her mother called for her. She carefully tucked the pamphlet away and scrambled to shove the tin behind the baseboard.

She walked to the door but hesitated, gripping the knob. Her heart raced but her head felt quiet and empty. She forced her legs to carry her to the kitchen to try a new dinner for her mother.

ACKNOWLEDGEMENTS

This is always the hardest piece to write, not because there's difficulty in naming people who shaped this work, but rather the innate fear that someone would be overlooked and left unwritten. Nothing ever happens in isolation, and Spectrum was no different. This was created and curated by a true collective and team.

Firstly and foremost, I express my gratitude to all the writers and creatives who gave us a piece of themselves. Whether or not you ended up in this anthology, you profoundly touched all of us with your vulnerability, authenticity, and strength. Your existence is a radical act of defiance of everything we stand against. Solidarity to you all, and all my strength to you finding homes for your creations.

Next, I want to thank La Mantia, the first person you saw when you picked up this book. Illustrators are too often overlooked, but they are our muse for the eyes, triggering parts of the brain our prose cannot. We entered this project as strangers, and now we leave as friends.

Furthermore, I want to thank Lor for their contributions as an editor and curator. Lor is an exceptional talent; the attention to detail is unparalleled. Their insight into body horror, a foreign genre, was illuminating. They were a joy to work with, and I can't wait to watch their star grow brighter and brighter with each passing day.

I want to thank Katherine Silva, who did the interior

formatting on Spectrum. You are an incredible talent, and your guiding hand has given this anthology the look and feel of something unlike what I have seen before. You, as always, are the consummate professional, and I can't wait to work further with you on many more projects.

I would also like to thank the Third Estate Board. This is our first release, the first paint stroke in a much broader canvas we hope to paint. Without the collective, this work would be impossible. There is solidarity in numbers, and each one of these board members fought tooth and nail to make this happen. I am deeply proud to know them and hope we can continue to serve the community with deep, meaningful, challenging art.

Lastly, I want to thank the community. I know not of what tomorrow brings of our space, but I know today was a good day. We shared a moment in time together; our eyes graced the same stories, and we could feel the power of the pen. We could feel the power of artists at work. I sincerely hope that somewhere in this book, something resonated with you. Connection to the world around us is the most meaningful thing anyone can achieve with their trip around the sun. For us Autistics, this can be a challenging and vulnerable thing. I will forever be your eternally grateful servant. It is the honor of a lifetime to curate this work. But the journey is only starting for us here, whether it's the Third Estate or these Authors who built this book with their bare hands. The first bricks are laid to a road unseen, but its gravity pulls us all forward.

This book is a radical act of defiance. Your existence is a radical act of defiance. Let's build a better world together.

One. Book. At. A. Time.

Long Live The Degeneracy,

Aquino Loayza

AUTHOR BIOS

Rain Corbyn is thrilled to have found a home in *Spectrum* for "Worry Your Head." Rain is an agender autistic person living on a wooded mountain. They write and narrate horror, romance, and erotica, delighting in the joy and horror of our bodies. Their narration has been nominated and a finalist for the Indie Ink Awards, and can be found on Audible. They narrate romance and smut as Richard Pendragon.

Adrian (he/they) is a queer and trans writer currently splitting his time between his rural Utah hometown and Boston, Massachusetts. "Like No Blood" combines his love for fellow trans people with his love for horror. When they aren't writing horror they are usually collaging or researching Great Lakes shipwrecks. They are a BFA Theatre Arts student, playwright, and opera stage manager at Boston University. You can find more of his work on Instagram, @adrianswrites.

Catherine Forrest (she/her), author of "These Thirteen Simple Tricks Will End Your Sleep Hallucinations for Good," is a writer, editor, and longtime sleep-disorder experiencer from Baltimore, Maryland. She produces medical publications by day and moonlights as the author of Shelf Life. Catherine currently lives in the suburbs of Baltimore with her partner and several furry and feathered pets.

Chris Nelson is the author of "A Dream So Sweet." He teaches at a Montessori school in Seattle, sometimes fails to be funny, is learning American Sign Language, and has begun work on his idealist metaphysical philosophy. His short fiction has appeared in *Andromeda Spaceways*, *Speculative North*, *Beyond the Bounds of Infinity*, and elsewhere.

Born and raised in the Philippines, **Caroline Hung** is a SFF writer of mixed Filipino and Taiwanese descent. She wrote her flash piece, "SURVIVE LOT 666," while stewing eyeballs-deep in an anxiety pool. See carolinehungauthor.com for more dreamy tales and incomprehensible auras.

Tim Lieder lives in Manhattan with his cats. "Discourses on the Seven Headed Monkey" was written while he was converting to Judaism. Additionally, he has published nine books through Dybbuk Press including *God Laughs When You Die* by Michael Boatman and *She Nailed a Stake Through his Head*. He's a professional student, ie: his day job involves writing term papers for lazy college students.

Die Booth, whose cautionary tale "Curse the Darkness" features in *Spectrum*, is a queer indie author who likes wild beaches and exploring dark places. When not writing, he DJs at Last Rites – the best (and only) goth club in Chester, UK. You can read his prize-winning stories in anthologies from *Egaeus Press*, *Neon Hemlock*, *Flame Tree Publishing* and many others. His books, including his charity collection *365 Lies*, horrordventure novel *Spirit Houses* and cursed sigil novella *Cool S* are available online. You can find out more about his writing at http://diebooth.wordpress.com/ or say hi on Instagram @ dieboothwrites or Bluesky @diebooth.bsky.social.

Akis comes from a version of Greece in a parallel universe. After the events of his story "The Sun Approaches Every Summer" he had to switch dimensions to escape heatstroke. He's a biomedical AI scientist who also conjures dark stories, some of which have wormed their way into *Apex, Dread*

Machine, *Flame Tree*, *Gamut Magazine* and other bloodied places. Visit his lair for more succulent tales from this world and others: https://linktr.ee/akislinardos

John Wiswell is an ace/aro writer who lives where New York keeps all its trees. He has won the Nebula Award for Best Short Story for "Open House on Haunted Hill," the Locus Award for Best Novelette for "That Story Isn't The Story," and his work has been translated into ten languages. His debut novel, *SOMEONE YOU CAN BUILD A NEST IN*, is forthcoming from *DAW Books* in April of 2024. As an ace person and a frequent migraine sufferer, "But The Wifi Is Great" is a deeply personal story. He wishes us all to find a little more relief.

Lucas Shipwright, arguably human, grew up in the Appalachian foothills and took all those ghost stories to heart. They enjoy writing unsettling tales that feel almost too personal, but "Given Names" is the first one lucky enough to be pressed to pages. You can find them and their other available works at linktr.ee/shipwrote.

Xochilt Avila (they/them) is a queer, non-binary, and multiracial author who currently resides in Maryland, USA. These experiences, living outside of binary labels, have helped foster their appreciation for the uncomfortable, the uneasily defined, and the unloved. Outside of horror, they love playing video games and tabletop RPGs, getting lost in the woods, and fulfilling the whims of their cats. They are immensely grateful for being a part of the *Spectrum* anthology. Follow them on Twitter @ahandfulofteeth, Instagram @ xochiltavilawrites, and @ahandfulofteeth.bsky.social.

Nexus Hope (they/them) is a queer neurodivergent graduate of Holyoke Community College (HCC) with a degree in creative writing and is currently studying literature at

Hampshire College, graduating in the Spring of 2024. Their short story, "The Thing That Lives in the House," is a creatively horrific interpretation of sensory overload. The terror of sound is very real and lurking behind every corner.

Steve Neal, author of "So, This is Freedom?", is a neurodivergent, English-born writer currently surviving the summers of Florida with his supportive wife and less supportive cats. As a lifelong horror fanatic, he enjoys poking at the unknown and seeing what comes crawling out, as long as it isn't spiders. His debut novella *TO LOVE A DYING WORLD* releases in 2025 through Off Limits Press. Follow him on Twitter @SteveNealWrites.

Sarah Musnicky is an autistic, disabled queer writer hailing from Los Angeles. When she's not balancing between film criticism and working in association management, she can be found snuggling her cat, Jupiter, who may or may not be a demon-in-disguise. If you ever see her in the wild, she accepts coffee offerings as it is her primary food source. Her latest short story, "The Mask it Wears," continues her dissection of boundaries and consent from an autistic POV, with a little Halloween Horror twist.

Olive is a 23 year old, non-binary, disabled lesbian who writes about young queer people finding hope even at the end of the world. When they're not writing, they can be found playing Nintendo games, watching Star Wars, or working as a barista. They attained their degree in creative writing, and currently live in Louisville, Kentucky with their wife, dog, and three cats.

Climber, tattoo collector, and peanut-butter connoisseur, **Xan van Rooyen** is an autistic, non-binary storyteller from South Africa, currently living in Finland where the heavy metal is soothing and the cold, dark forests inspiring. Xan has a

Master's degree in music, and—when not teaching—enjoys conjuring strange worlds and creating quirky characters. You can find Xan's stories in the likes of *Three-Lobed Burning Eye*, *Daily Science Fiction*, and *Galaxy's Edge* among others. They have also written several novels including YA fantasy *My Name is Magic*, and adult arcanepunk novel *Silver Helix*. Xan is also part of the Sauutiverse, an African writer's collective with their first anthology *Mothersound* out now from *Android Press*.

Ashley Lezak (they/she) is a disabled author of uncomfortable works. They live in Washington State with their husband and two ridiculous rescue dogs, where they spend their time reading, crocheting, gardening, and fighting with insurance companies. Their work has appeared as "Adrift" in *Negative Space 2: A Return to Survival Horror* and as "Different" in *Spectrum: An Autistic Horror Anthology*.

Jonathan La Mantia creates detailed and sometimes chaotic ink works as a way to process the infinite horrors of our world, both external and internal. They have been living in isolation with their partner since March 21, 2020 and are currently working to further develop their artistic voice as a more conscious representation of their disabled, AuDHD, trans and queer identity.

Lor Gislason is a writer and occasional editor from Vancouver Island, Canada. Ask them about their current hyperfixation or their cat Pierogi Platter and they'll love you forever.

Aquino Loayza is a Queer Latino author from the Boston Area. *Deep* is their Debut Novel. Aquino has always been drawn horror, and deeper societal themes. Outside of writing, Aquino enjoys traveling and experiencing the peculiar, strange, and otherwise overlooked. They live with their wife and pug in rural Massachusetts.

TRIGGER WARNINGS

Worry Your Head: gore, dismemberment, misgendering, animal death, religious trauma

Like No Blood: death, animal death, blood/gore, needles, death of a loved one

Thirteen Simple Tricks: mention of violence, mention of needles

A Dream So Sweet: grief, loss of a loved one, violence, mentioned child violence

Survive Lot 666: animal post-mortem

Discourses of the Seven-Headed Monkey: gore, animal horror, body horror

Curse The Darkness: suicide, intrusive thoughts, depression

The Sun Approaches Every Summer: burning and associated horror

But The Wi-Fi Is Great: migraines, gaslighting

Given Names: body horror, gore

Safe Food: misgendering, deadnaming, gore, death

So, This Is Freedom?: self-harm, body hatred, blood, implied bigotry

The Mask It Wears: violence

Bitemark Bitch: descriptions of gore, obsession, implied sexual content

Neighborly: sexual content, gore, murder, paranoia

The Silence of Broken Things: death of a loved one, grief

Different: unconsented conversion therapy